A SEA AMONG STARS

An oceans-themed anthology
compiled by Nathaniel Luscombe and Cheyenne van Langevelde

This book is a work of fiction. Any references to historical events, real people, or real places are used fictitiously. Other names, characters, places, and events are products of the author's imagination, and any resemblance to actual events or places or persons, living or dead, is currently coincidental.

Copyright © 2023 Nathaniel Luscombe and Cheyenne van Langevelde

All rights reserved, including the right of reproduction in whole or in part in any form.

ISBN: 979-8-9883213-0-9

TABLE OF CONTENTS

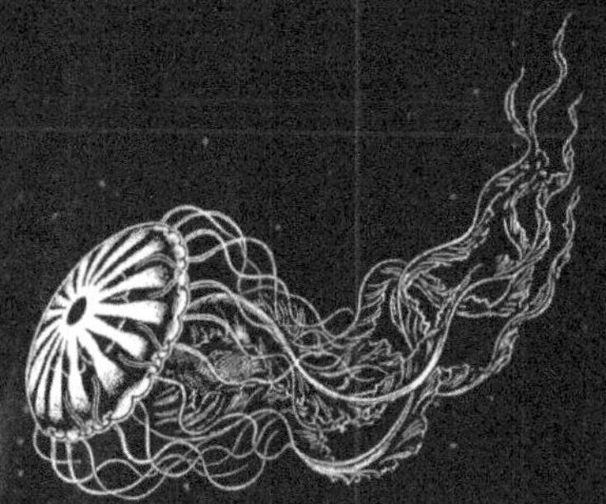

WHITE STARS

shadows dig in salt water
a creature come alive
a mix of polaris and diabase
that's soon to make you thrive

these stars are endless in their spread
moonstone cutting off the notion
that in every breath you take
you will find white-stars in the ocean

Erelah Emerson

SIREN SONG

Anna Augustine

Chapter One

I am stranded in space.

I stare out at the vast expanse, fear clenching my chest as the swirling purples, blues, and pinks of a galaxy wink around my worthless starship. Our lightleaper is dead, rendered useless, though not by any fault of our own. But that means an entire ship of space cadets may die.

I turn to Guppy, my first mate. His gills open and close in measured beats as his bulbous eyes scan the stars before us. He has mastered the art of expressionless calm.

"This is bad, Ambrose." His speech is somewhat garbled, like listening to a person speaking while underwater.

"You don't think I know that?" I snap, roughing a hand over my face. I turn to the navigation pad, bracing my arms on either side of it as I stare at the blinking red light that marks our position in the infinite starfield. "We had to run into that pod of whales, didn't we? Nothing can ever be easy for Starship Thirteen."

"I think the number should have been an indicator." Guppy smirks, his webbed hand gesturing to the pad. "I have no idea if we can make it home, but here"—he points to a cluster of stars on the pad—"is…well it's…"

"Spit it out," I growl, my hands fisting at my side.

"It's the siren colony, sir."

"You've got to be joking! What they trade goes against the laws of the Starfleet. Why would I go to them for help?"

Guppy shrugs. "Our lightleaper is dead, Captain. We have next to no fuel, and our only viable option is to trade with the sirens for the fuel to get this ship home. It's one man versus an entire crew."

"But it's never a fair trade," I grumble, looking down from the flight deck to the crew below. They're furiously typing on their pads and control boards, looking for some way to get home. I see mothers and fathers. Sisters and brothers. Sons and daughters.

The life of a space cadet is never guaranteed. They know that the day they sign up. But something in me always hates it. Hates holding the life of these people in my hands. One choice—one decision—could kill hundreds. It's one I don't hold lightly.

"We will trade with the sirens. But the sirens don't have a choice on who they get." I turn to Guppy. "I'll trade myself for the fuel you'll need to get home."

"Captain—"

I hold up my hand. "If they won't trade it for me, we will all die together. The old saying is a captain always goes down *with* his ship. Why not for it, eh?"

Guppy's gills flap faster, as if he wants to argue with me. But he should know by now that arguing is worthless. Once I've made up my mind, few can stop me.

He grasps the navigation pad, glaring at me as he punches in the coordinates. I sit down in my captain's chair, watching the twisting galaxy that belongs to the sirens as it draws ever nearer. We start to see movement among the stars. They aren't as deadly as many think. Oh, for humans, space would suck the life out of us, choking us in its iron-like grip as we slowly turn to ice.

But the sirens aren't human. Though they're not like the mermaids of Earth, either. They're special. Magical. Dangerous. Deadly. And humans are their favorite prey, tokens they trade for whatever the rest need. They're tricky and good at what they do.

The tightness in my chest worsens as we bank to the starboard side and reach the star cluster. The shadows lengthen between the stars, the shifting movements of tails and scales glinting in the faint light. Just beyond it, a black hole swirls, the doorway to the kingdom of the sirens. I stand, stalking over to the large glass windows and press my palm against it.

"Everybody, out of this room!" I order. My crew gapes at me but obey with silent looks of concern.

I ignore them. I have to. This is my only chance to save them all.

One man for the entire crew.

Guppy remains standing by the control pad. He grew up in the siren world; he can breathe in the vacuum of space, but I don't want him to see me as I know I will become. I clench my hands at my side, angry that it has come to this.

A fist pounds against the window and I nearly startle back. A soulless creature floats outside. Obsidian eyes stare back at me from a face that's all sharp lines. The siren's lifeless gray hair floats around him as if he's underwater. Its iridescent black tail flicks back and forth as it stares at me, head cocked.

I force myself to stand straight and meet the haunting gaze as I say, "I need fuel for my ship and I'm willing to trade for it."

The siren lists to the left as he lifts his willowy arm and taps his gnarled finger against the glass, coding out a sentence.

I. Want. You.

I raise a brow in surprise. That was surprising, though it could have been that there was simply no one else in the command room for him to barter for besides Guppy.

"I am the captain of this vessel," I state.

The siren smiles, causing chills to run up and down my arms. He was beautifully haunting, a lifeless form of beauty floating through the void of space. He raises his hand again and my stomach sours as he taps out, *Yes. And. My. Sister. Needs. A. Mate.*

Guppy lets out his bubbly laugh, but it's a flat sound. "This is more than you bargained for, isn't it?"

It is. I had sworn off marriage. Off women. My whole life was about the Starfleet. My crew often said I was married to my work, and that was true. I love space. I love my planet. They had become my family, my love, the thing I turned to when the world was spinning out of control. Can I really give it all up to save my crew?

But if I don't, we are all doomed to die regardless. I am willing to sacrifice everything that matters to me if it means keeping the cadets on this ship safe.

With my hands fisted at my side, and hoping I'm not making a grave mistake, I say, "I accept."

That cold smile twists the siren's lips again and he tips his head back, letting out a piercing screech. The glass trembles but doesn't break. I turn to Guppy, nodding once, and he clicks the release button.

The window rises up, the vacuum tugging at everything. Papers scatter, alarms blare, I gasp. Choking from the lack of oxygen, I am tugged out into space. Perhaps it is the lack of air, but the colors seem brighter here. The pinks have a hotness to them while the blues are numbingly frigid. They dance across my exposed skin in waves. I want to scream, but I can't move.

The siren floats up to me, clicking his tongue in a strange language I can't understand. His twisted fingers reach out, clamping over my bicep. It burns worse than the colors, sending fire through my veins.

I try to twist away from it, but the siren holds fast, dragging me through the star clusters and toward the black hole. I still cannot breathe, my vision blurring as the pain and choking increases. A flash of light surrounds us before the blackness edging my vision envelops me completely.

Chapter Two

I blink awake with a jerk, groaning as my limbs ache. My skin is frigid and my teeth clatter as I sit up. Dizziness claims me as the disorientation worsens. Everything has dimmed around me—the colors, the lights, and yes, the temperature. I try to move my legs, a strange tingling drawing my eyes to them. My throat closes off as I see…

A tail.

I knew the price would be steep. I had chosen to sacrifice myself to save my crew. But I wasn't expecting this.

Unlike the siren who captured me, my tail glitters shades of green in the faint light. From turquoise to sage to forest emerald, it is beautiful. I look around, seeing open arches of white stone that reveal more colors of the rainbow beyond as the stars wink against it. Reds blend with the pinks, yellows and greens swirling among the blue. It is stunning. I flick my tail, rising up ever so slightly from the bed I'm on. I shiver, but more from the strange sensation than the cold.

A shadow moves on my right. Turning, I see the siren I had traded myself to. But he is different now. Gone are the grays and blacks that had covered him. He nearly glows, his skin pale and flawless. He moves closer, his tail shimmering in the dim light that catches the pearly white by his waist to the navy blue of his fins. His deep hair waves through the air, once more reminding me of swimming in the seas of Earth.

"Good, you're awake." His voice is low and not garbled like Guppy's usually is. Is it because I'm a siren now too?

"Where… Where am I?" My chest still aches, but it's a dull throb. I rub at it, realizing my chest is as bare as his.

"You're in Raelithion, home of the merfolk." He smiles a tight-lipped smirk, but his dark brown eyes are hard. "Though I believe your kind refer to us as sirens."

"You look…different." I cough, my throat raw. It must have been the screaming or the lack of air as I'd been pulled through the vacuum of space.

"I am the same as I have always been." He glides to my side now. "It's only that your perception of me has changed."

"What?" I rub at my temple, my head starting to pound.

"Lie back down," he orders. I submit without a fight, dizziness making me feel nauseous. "Your transformation is still fresh. You need to recover your strength before the wedding."

"Wedding?" I jerk up, my tail fluttering. "What wedding?"

"You promised your hand in exchange for fuel. You're marrying my sister."

"Wait, wait!" I groan as the room starts to spin, and I lie back down. "I haven't even met her."

He raises a brow, his arms crossing over his chest. "Are you breaking your vow? One word from me, and my army can decimate your ship."

"No, no. Please." I cover my face with my hands. Exhaustion presses down on me again. I swallow, everything rising and falling in me like the tide. "Can I meet her?"

Silence.

I lower my hands to find the strange siren is gone. I shiver again, looking to see if there is a blanket, but there's nothing around that will warm me. Besides, this cold is coming from the inside out. I sigh, gazing up at the vaulted ceiling.

A shadow falls over me, and I turn my head to see a stunning siren at my side.

Her hair is a light pink, cascading around her pale shoulders. A strapless, aqua shirt wraps around her torso, ending a few inches above a magenta tail. Like her brother's, it is paler at the waist, turning darker as it goes down. The scales shimmer as she swims closer.

"You're the one I'm stuck with?" Her nose wrinkles in distaste. "Pathetic."

"Excuse me?" I push to my elbows, glaring at her.

"Listen, my father has tried marrying me off to every merman in our kingdom. Some even a few galaxies beyond. None of them could handle my fabulous personality." She flicks her hair over her shoulder, smirking at me. "So, what makes you any different?"

"I-I—" I shake my head, regretting that action almost immediately. "Nothing. I'm…nothing special. I gave myself to your people to save a ship full of my own. I truly expected to die the moment that window opened. I don't understand what is happening to me." I cover my face again as the room spins. I struggle to slow my breathing before I have a panic attack in front of the merwoman.

"You sacrificed yourself for your people?" she asks slowly.

"Yes," I mumble.

"Hm."

"Vera!" The first siren swims up to his sister, his gaze hot as he glares at me. "You're marrying him. He's your last choice."

"Did I say I wasn't marrying him, Oran?" she snaps. "No, I'll do what Father and you tell me. But I shan't make it fun for him." Her grin is nearly wicked as she turns and swims out of the room.

Oran flicks his tail in agitation, turning to me once more with his arms crossed over his chest. "Good luck with her."

"You said her name is Vera?" I ask weakly, in no mood to argue with my captors.

"Yes. What is it they call you, human?"

"I'm Ambrose." I close my eyes, the exhaustion pressing down relentlessly.

"Good name." Oran grunts. "Let's hope you can live up to its legacy."

I jerk awake, my dreams of choking on space air, freezing to death in the vacuum of space vanishing. Part of me hoped I'd wake up aboard my starship, all of the sirens and whales and monsters a horrid nightmare from one-too-many cups of grog.

But I'm still in the white room, the rainbow of stars on the other side. I flick my tail, my brain somehow knowing how to pilot me, and I swim through the air to the large arches. I sag against the column, my throat tight at the beauty just out of reach.

Below me is a city. Towers of white and gray and brown spiral up, the pointed tops all carrying the emblem of a trident. I am in a tower myself, high above the merfolk gliding through the streets and in and out of the buildings below me. I stick my hand out of the arch, yanking it back as cold clings to it.

Magic must keep the buildings warm, I think. I barely feel anything at this revelation. But then I glance down at my tail. Disbelief blurs my vision. I can't be a siren. That's not how it works. One doesn't simply turn into a merman.

"Shock is common, though I must say, you're handling it extremely well."

I turn toward the voice. An ancient-looking siren swims closer, his orange tail gleaming. Like Oran, his chest is bare, though his skin is many shades darker. It also holds the mark of time. His long white beard and hair shiver through the air. His golden eyes twinkle and he smiles at me, lessening some of the tension that has coiled around my neck and shoulders.

"Sir, I don't understand what is happening." I gesture around and then down at my tail, my words fleeing me.

"Again, 'tis normal." He clasps my shoulder. "My name is Bacus, the Ancient One of the Merfolk."

"*Ancient One?*" I give him a look of skepticism. "Really?"

He chuckles, unaffected by my tone. "Yes, young Ambrose, that is my title."

I cross my arms, still feeling chilled. "Where am I?"

"You are in Raelithion, as Prince Oran told you earlier."

He motions for me to follow, and I do. It's jerky, but I manage, until something the man said pulls me up short.

"Wait. *Prince* Oran? Meaning that Vera is…"

"Vera is *Lady* Vera. She is Oran's half-sister." A sour look twists Bacus' face. "Her mother was…less than scrupulous."

I wince. "If Vera is anything like her mother in personality, I can see that."

Bacus' brows raise in amusement. "Best not say that to her, my boy."

I shrug, crossing my arms as I follow Bacus out the door.

The halls are the same white stone, but they have swirls and patterns on them. The colors match the beautiful ones I had seen in the sky. They depict scenes of mermaids and mermen swimming—for there was no other word to describe the fluid movements—among the stars and planets. Some show the merfolk dancing with one another to music I can't hear, yet feel inside my very bones. I gape, numb to it all.

A dream. This has to be a dream.

"Where are we going?" I ask Bacus as I follow him into the street.

The merfolk stop and stare at me. A handful whisper to each other and my face burns. Apparently, I am the spectacle of the hour.

"We are heading to the temple." He grins over his shoulder. "It's your wedding day."

I stop. My throat closes off. I can see the Starfleet command center and the vows I made to fulfill my duties to them and them alone fill my mind. That day, I also swore off marriage. Women. Temptations and distractions. I chose the life of a Starfleet captain. I can't marry anyone, let alone another species.

"No," I whisper.

"You vowed it." Bacus morphs before me, his eyes turning dark and hollow, his orange tail bleeding into gray. "You will keep your vow or suffer my wrath!"

"All right! All right!" I hold up my hands, shaking my head to clear my vision. "I…if I must."

"You must, young Ambrose." I blink and Bacus is back to the way he looked before. His eyes, the strangest shade of gold, sparkle. "It's been prophesied."

"Wait, what?" I ask in bewilderment as I hurry to catch up with the merman. "There's a prophecy?"

"Yes." He doesn't elaborate, simply says, "But no more talk. No one's destiny is ever achieved by knowing their supposed future."

"You said it was about me. Doesn't that mean it's going to happen?"

"Ah, but there's the way you *think* it is going to happen and the way it *is* going to happen." Bacus smiled at me. "Those are two very different things, my boy."

I sigh, staring at the towering temple we've stopped in front of. Three spires twist up into the purple sky, encased in gold. The emblem of the trident glows against the double doors that are set in the same white stone that is popular here. It takes everything in me to follow Bacus through them.

The aisle is long and plain. The stone benches on either side are empty. A raised platform sits at the end, three merpeople waiting at its base. All turn to face Bacus and me as we move towards them. One of the figures is Prince Oran, the other is Lady Vera, and the last figure is the most imposing one of all.

Of all the merfolk I've met thus far, he is the most muscular. On his wrists are two golden cuffs with swirling runes etched on them. A five-pronged crown rests on his head, curly brown hair that matches Oran's flowing to his shoulders. His tail is also blue, but darker in the shades. A trident rests in his hand and he points it at me when Bacus and I reach the platform.

"I shall test the truth of this young space sailor before he weds Vera."

"Of course." I throw back my shoulders, trying to still the tremble in my hands. "Ask away."

A bemused smile graces the king's face. "Why are you here, sailor?"

"I exchanged myself for fuel. I wanted my crew to reach Earth and their families once more." I clasp my hands behind me as the trident begins to glow. The warmth of it covers me, making me the warmest I've been since arriving. Sparkles dance around before it fades. Something burns on my bicep, and I glance at it.

A rune is on my arm. What it means, I don't know. But triumph fills me at the sight of it. I turn toward the king and bow. "I do not wish to cause problems in your kingdom, sire. I only wished for my people to be safe."

"And they shall be." The king nods. "I, King Theon of Raelithion, vow that this man's crew shall not be harmed. And neither shall he."

Bacus clasps my shoulder. "Shall we begin the ceremony?"

King Theon nods, motioning for Vera to join hands with me. The mermaid glares, her eyes frosty. They are the most peculiar shade of purple, light and airy but as cold as ice as she looks at me.

Bacus begins the wedding ceremony. I barely hear him, so focused am I on breathing as panic chokes me. I know my hands are trembling, but I can't seem to stop them. Vera keeps glancing at me with her cold gaze, and it takes everything in me not to swim far, far away. Maybe it would have been better to die in space than marry a siren.

"Do you, Ambrose of Earth, swear to remain faithful and true to Vera of Raelithion? To guard her heart like the holy stars, to relish in its light and to never try to dim it? Do you vow to listen to its guidance, to fight the shadows that wish to overcome it, and to cherish it for the power and might it holds within?"

The vows stir something in me. I turn to Vera, who still looks angry at marrying me, and feel a tug, a song like the one that has floated around the pictures in the hallway. A siren song. A dangerous lure used to ensnare sailors. But I cannot ignore it.

"I do," I state boldly. The panic flees as peace settles around me. This was what was meant to happen.

"And do you, Vera of Raelithion, swear to remain faithful and true to Ambrose of Earth? To guard his heart like the holy stars, to relish in its light and to never try to dim it? Do you vow to listen to its guidance, to fight the shadows that wish to overcome it, to cherish it for the power and might it holds within," Bacus hesitates, before adding, "and to follow him as he embarks on a path not of his choosing?"

Vera's brows lower in puzzlement. She turns toward me, something searching in her gaze. Her mouth opens and closes a few times before she whispers, "I do."

Bacus motions for King Theon to approach. The trident glows, wrapping a band of gold around our joined hands. A warmth buzzes through me once again, up my arm and into my chest. I gasp, my grip tightening on Vera's hand.

"I bind thee as one, from this day on, forevermore!" Bacus raises his hands, his gold eyes bright in the light from the trident. "It is finished."

The light abruptly cuts off and Vera drops my hand. I blink as I gaze at it. Swirls and runes cover the back of my hand, shimmering in the faint light around me. I glance at Vera's hand and see identical patterns.

Like the wedding bands on Earth? I shiver and turn toward my bride. "What now?"

"Now I will take you to our rooms." She sounds less than pleased, and I swallow the snarky retort I want to spit at her. Instead, I offer her my hand, which she promptly ignores. I follow after her, but not before I hear a snigger from Oran.

This…is going to be interesting.

Chapter Three

I'm huffing by the time we reach Vera's—our—room. She flings open the door, letting it hit the wall as she swims to the bed and flops onto it with a dramatic sigh. I raise my brow, closing the door and leaning against it.

"That was quite the entrance." I deadpan. It breaks into a smirk when she glares at me. "I know you don't like me, Vera, but I'm not sure why."

"Because you were human." She waves her hand at me. "I get enough disdain because of what my mother did. I am very fortunate that Theon treats me as his own. But I'm not a princess, and all the merfolk know it. It was an abomination, what my mother did, and I live with that scorn. Now, I'm married to a *human*-turned-merman. That's not common, Ambrose."

"Well, where I'm from, you're a terror. A horror story told to young children who won't go to bed at night. So, I guess I'm an abomination married to a terror."

She scoffs, but a small smile tugs on her lips. "I suppose so."

Silence reigns and I have to stifle a yawn. The room is very…pink. The bed where Vera sits is covered in a pale pink bedspread. Pink curtains and paintings hang along the walls, while chairs upholstered in a magenta fabric sit around a round stone circle. A light blue flame sparks at its center, and I move towards it, curious.

"What is this?" I ask, reaching toward it.

"Don't touch it!" Vera hurries to yank my arm away, a scowl on her face. "It's our heat source. Warms the buildings we live in."

I feel it now, the heat rising around the circle taking the chill away that's been hanging on me since I turned.

"Amazing," I breathe, a little awestruck. "Your world is…amazing."

Vera rolls her eyes. "It has its flaws."

"Like every world does." I shrug, sitting back in the chair I've claimed, my tail lazily floating up and down in an invisible current. "But that doesn't make them any less stunning. It only means there's work to be done."

Vera studies me again, like I'm a giant puzzle she can figure out if she only thinks hard enough. "What is Earth like?"

And so we talk. We talk about Earth, about our customs and foods and sports. She tells me about Raelithion as the servants bring us a meal of strange— but not horrible—food. She shares about the merfolk as I tell her the myths surrounding them.

"But…why did I see Oran as a…a siren?" I ask, finishing off a piece of what she called *patapay*. Flakey and moist, it closely resembles a chocolate-filled croissant from Earth.

"You humans see what you want to see." Vera takes a bite of her *patapay*, chewing slowly as she thinks. "You see us as monsters, so we are."

"But why aren't you monsters now?" I ask in bewilderment.

"You are one of us. You gained a new perception when that happened. No longer are we different to you; we are one." A pretty pink blush stole into her pale cheeks. "I am sorry for being cross before the wedding."

"Why are you apologizing?" I lick a glob of the chocolate-type substance off my fingers. "I was no happier than you were."

Vera cocks her head, her pink hair falling over her shoulder. "Why?"

"I vowed I would never wed." I fidget with the napkin in my lap. "My work kept me busy. It wasn't fair to saddle a woman with that work as well."

"Do mates on Earth not work together?"

"Not usually. Sometimes women work, but rarely do men and women work in the same place together."

"Strange, that." Vera trails her finger around the interact carvings on the armrest of the chair. "Here, once a couple weds, the woman serves with the man in whatever job he does. If he is a soldier, they serve together. An advisor, the man serves the king, while the wife works with the queen. They are stronger together." She weaves her fingers together, the corners of her mouth tipping up the slightest bit. She stares at her hands for a long moment before shaking herself and looking up at me once more. "I wish to know what it was like as a starship captain."

"It was not nearly as grand as they make it out to be." I smile. "Lots of work, low pay, disgusting food. But I got to see the galaxies, make new friends, and boss people around."

"Bossing people helps you make friends?" Vera smirks.

I return it with a shrug and a cocky tilt of my head. "Some of the time. My first mate put up with me, at least." At the thought of Guppy, my chest tightens. I stare down at my tail, sweeping it across the titled ground. I feel as though more needs to be said, but I'm all out of words.

Vera twirls a strand of her hair around her finger. "You're different from many of the humans who've come here, Ambrose."

"Is that good?" I ask weakly, slumping against the chair. My head is drained of words, my body sagging in exhaustion that pulls on my eyelids. It takes all my willpower to force myself to meet Vera's gaze.

"Possibly." She taps her other hand against her chin. "I have a feeling you'll be something special."

"To you, my lady?" I can't help goading her a bit, and the blush in her cheeks is very worth it.

She tosses her hair over her shoulder and shrugs. "Now *that* remains to be seen."

Vera claims one side of the bed, shoving me to the other with an icy glare that promises pain if I try anything. Not that I want to. I close my eyes, but despite my exhaustion, sleep eludes me. Visions of Oran and space tighten my chest as I try to grasp the slippery bonds of rest.

After a few hours of restless tossing and turning, I swim to the window. There's no glass in it, and I lean my arms against the sill. A strange breeze–maybe a current of some kind–brushes my blond hair across my forehead and I sigh. Bacus' words at the wedding, my talk with Vera, Oran's obvious disdain—they swirl and blend in my mind as I lean my head against the window's edge.

A prophecy? I scratch my cheek. Why would I be a prophecy? And why wouldn't they tell me about it?

I glance over at Vera. She's curled on her side, a thin blanket tucked under her chin. Her hair frames her face. She's peaceful, the hardness of her features and the tension in her shoulders gone as she slumbers. Would she tell me the truth?

There's the way you think it is going to happen and the way it is going to happen. Bacus' words tickle my mind. *Those are two very different things, my boy.*

I snort softly, growling at the thought of being left in the dark.

A gong echoes down the hall, startling me as I turn toward it. Vera groans, throwing the blanket over her head as I swim back to the bed.

"What's happening?"

"It's the signal to rise for the morning meal." She mutters something else, but it's lost in the blanket.

"Are you not a morning person?" I ask, as I carefully grip the end of her hiding place between my fingers.

"No."

I chuckle before yanking hard. The blanket floats to the ground as an irate Vera pins me with her frosty gaze. I smile and some emotion I can't name flicks across her face.

"Rise and shine!" I chirp.

"What?"

"It's…well, it's a human saying."

Vera stares at me blankly for so long I start to squirm. The left side of her mouth finally quirks up. "That's a strange saying. *Rise and shine.* How does one shine, Ambrose?"

My name on her tongue sends a strange thrill through me, and I force myself to clasp my hands behind my back. "I suppose they might shine if one swallowed some beams of light. Imagine their fingers glowing."

I wiggle them at her and she laughs slightly. It sounds like tiny bells, light and airy and beautiful. I have the sudden desire to make her laugh every day.

With a cough, I choke my own breath at *that* particular line of thinking. I'd known this woman all of two days. Married for less than that.

"Well, it's time to eat." She swims over to me, placing her hand in mine. "You'll escort me, of course."

"Of course," I state, though it was a statement, not a question.

Vera begins to swim, and I follow, a lump settling in my throat at the thought of eating in the presence of King Theon and Prince Oran. Vera was becoming comfortable after our night of talking, but her family was another matter entirely

We soon reach two massive doors. A guard is positioned in front of them, not even his tail moving as he stands straight and tall. He barely blinks as we glide up and halt before him. Snapping his fingers, he swims to the side. For a moment, nothing happens. I open my mouth to ask Vera about it when the doors suddenly whisper open without a soul touching them.

"Incredible," I mutter, eyeing them as we swim through.

Vera smiles up at me, though it's almost mocking. "Are we as abominable as you humans think?"

I scoff softly, a teasing grin on my face as I lean down to whisper, "No, no, no. I'm the abomination and you're the terror. Remember our talk last night?"

She laughs, a genuine smile on her face as I guide her to the table. We're the first ones here and she shows me where to sit.

We've only just situated ourselves when the doors ghost open once more. Prince Oran enters with an older mermaid on his arm. Her brown hair, streaked with gray, is done up atop her head. She has on an orange top, thin bands running over her shoulders. Her tail is a solid yellow, with no variation as the other merpeople I've met have. Her appraisal of me is full of disdain as she sniffs and lets Oran set her beside the chair at the head of the table.

The Queen of Raelithion.

"So," the woman's voice is deep and husky, her blue eyes sharp as she pierces me, "you're the poor sop who got stuck with the whore's daughter, eh?"

"Mother!" Oran's voice is filled with barely masked fury, his face holding a large amount of disbelief. His knuckles go white as his large hands grip the back of the queen's seat.

"What?" Her voice is full of insincere innocence. "It's the truth, son. You know this."

"Vera is my sister," he grinds out between clenched teeth. "Apologize."

"No." The queen sniffs and actually turns her nose up at Vera. "I don't think I will."

My eyes dart to Vera at my side. Her gaze has dropped to her lap, her fingers tracing her scales. Was her chin trembling?

Fierce protection wells within me and I glare at the queen. "I don't care who you are, that was unacceptable."

Vera's head whips up, her eyes wide at my outburst.

But I am not done. "Vera is my wife. We vowed to never let the shadows overcome the other's light. You've attempted that with your words." I rise, bracing my fists on the table. "Apologize to my wife. Now."

The room is so quiet, I wonder if everyone is frozen. But I don't let my gaze waver from the witch of a mermaid before me. Her jaw stiffens but she turns to Vera. "I apologize."

Vera nods at her stepmother before gripping my wrist and yanking me back into the chair. Oran swims around and claims the seat beside his sister, but a thoughtful look lingers in his eyes as he meets my gaze.

"Well, this is a quiet group." King Theon swims in from a side door. His gaze sweeps us all, furrowing only slightly when they land on Vera, whose head has bowed once more. He swims over to the queen, kissing the top of her head, "Good morning, Ula."

She grunts, her sullen look spearing me. I smile coolly, and if King Theon notices, he says nothing.

Once the king claims his seat, he claps his hands once. "Let's eat."

The servants swim in and out, passing out our morning meal. I'm pleased to find more *patapay* among the dishes served. There's also a warm vanilla pudding that Vera tells me is called *resern*. Whatever it is, I love it. I eat without speaking, watching Queen Ula from time to time. Her scowl doesn't lessen. King Theon tries to engage her in conversation, but she ignores him.

The tension crackles through the air, and you would have to be a fool to miss it. And King Theon is no fool. He pushes his plate away and raises his thick brows, glancing from Oran to Vera then over to me. "What happened?"

"What do you mean?" Ula asks with the same insincere tone she used when insulting Vera.

"Before I came in. What happened?"

Oran points at Ula. "She insulted Vera. Again."

"He's lying, Theo! Why would I insult your daughter?"

Theon's daughter. Not Ula's. I rub my chin, thinking through what Vera shared the night before. *Interesting dynamic.*

"It's fine, Oran." The spark in Vera's words and expression that had been there when we first met is gone. It's almost as if a bucket of water dosed it. "Leave it be."

"No." I grab her arm, shaking my head. "It's not all right."

"Stop!" she hisses, shooting me a look full of pleading, and I clamp my lips together.

"Why do you never believe me?" Ula crosses her arms, a pout on her thin lips.

Theon raises a brow. "Because you have a track record of lying."

My mouth drops a little at that bit of bluntness but I swiftly snap it closed.

"What happened, Ambrose?" Theon turns to me.

I turn to Vera, who won't meet my gaze. "Your wife called Vera names that…well, they were rather crass." Heat swirls in my gut. "I made her apologize to Vera, your majesty."

"Really?" Surprise laces his words and when both Oran and I nod, one side of his mouth rises in a smile. "Well done."

"Truly?" I ask.

Theon laughs, deep and throaty. "You stood up for my daughter. Yes, well done."

I smile, wondering if I look as dazed as I feel. Nodding toward the king, I pop another bite of *patapay* into my mouth.

"May we be excused, Father?" Vera asks, and when he nods, she grabs my wrist and hauls me out of the dining room.

"What was that?" she snaps the moment we are clear of any lingering ears.

I cross my arms over my chest, raising a brow at her. "What was what?"

She fists her hands on her hips. "You ordered Queen Ula to apologize! Do you know how miserable she can make my life?"

"She hurt you." My hand twitches. I want to cup her cheek in my hand, but judging by the anger in her eyes, she'd quite possibly bite my hand off if I attempt it. "I saw the way your fire dimmed when she called you what she did."

Vera's voice cracks as she whispers, "Because I am what she called me, Ambrose. I am the spawn of a whore."

I move closer. "You are who *you* are, Vera. You're not your parents' mistakes."

She drops her gaze. "You know nothing about me, Ambrose."

"But I want to." I dare to tip her chin up. "I want to know everything about you."

Something warm sparks in my chest, traveling down my arm to ignite the brand on my arm. I hiss, grabbing at my shoulder as the heat grows in its intensity.

Vera's eyes widen, her hand clasping over mine. "Your truth brand!"

"My what?" I raise a brow.

"That mark that appeared when Father tested you yesterday." Her gaze drags from my shoulder to my eyes. Her voice drops as she whispers, "It means you're telling the truth."

I smile, nodding as another flash of pain heats my shoulder. It hurts. But then, I suppose the truth always does.

Vera presses her lips into a thin line, but the corners of her mouth quirks up. "Come."

I follow her through the halls, out into an open courtyard. Stopping short, my eyes grow round at the sight before me. Small star-shaped dots lay out like flowers in a field. Solid blackness is rippling beneath us, no stars breaking up its endlessness.

My eyes catch onto the smallest glowing dots. They're barely bigger than my pinkie and are ruby red. I lean down, scooping it into my palm. It flickers in my hand, barely warming my palm. A low hum rings around me and when I turn to look at Vera, she's spinning in a circle, light blue star dust clinging to her pink hair. Their pitch is slightly higher, blending with the bass hum of the red to create a beautiful melody.

Vera's eyes slide closed as yellow stars dot her face. Their note is higher still, rising and falling to add the melody.

The stars are drawn to the light in her, I realize. The red dot in my palm dances up to my cheek, settling against my nose. More of the red stars rise up, brushing my face, my arms, my chest. I chuckle, and their light and music grows.

It warms me. The chill that's come since my turning dissipates and I sigh in contentment.

I open my eyes as Vera slides up to me, wrapping her hand in mine. "Are you enjoying this?"

I nod. "I always knew that space was beautiful, but this…"

My voice trails off and Vera pulls me in farther. "The star fields are my favorite place in the whole of Raelithion. There is something comforting that, even in the vastness and the darkness of this place, light still shines."

"You shine." I glance down at her, smiling. "Despite the darkness all around you. You are fire and strength."

Vera snorts. "Pretty words, Ambrose."

"But they're true." I tug her further into the star field. "And the stars never lie."

Purple sparks shimmer up, clinging to Vera's tail. Then green swirl around us both, settling in our hair and against our lips. I swing Vera in a circle to the music of the stars, though I'm not certain she can hear it. She gasps, a smile splitting her face as I laugh.

"See?" I pant as I stop, gazing up at the dancing lights. "They think you're something special. Just like me."

Vera chuckles, pushing me away. "You still don't know me."

"I don't need to know you well to see you're special." I drop her hands, shrugging as disappointment settles against my shoulders as she retreats from my embrace. "But I'm just an abomination. What do I know?"

Her brow furrows as I turn and swim back to the door. My heart aches, and I grasp at it with a gasp.

"Ambrose, are you okay?" Vera settles her hand between my shoulder blades.

"Fine," I grind out, squeezing my eyes shut as the pain fades.

"Where are you going?"

"Do you have a library?" I turn toward her.

"Yes?" Her brows lower in puzzlement. "Why?"

"I want to learn about my prophecy."

Chapter Four

The library is less than impressive.

A single shelf holds scrolls while another holds ten bound books. They face opposite each other, with a leather-bound tome on a pedestal in the center. The smell that envelops me and Vera is stale: old ink and parchment swirling on the dusty air. I sneeze and she snickers.

"This is it?" I question, unable to hide the disappointment.

"Yes." Vera sighs. "It was all that was saved when we fled here."

"Fled?" I ask, turning to see the sorrow lining her mouth.

"I was six when the marauders attacked our old home in the Quaso sector. That home was hidden by a black hole and no one bothered us. Our population was nearly double what it is now." She crosses her arms, catching her lip between her teeth.

"How'd they find you?"

"A traitor." Vera rubs her bare arms as she shivers. "When the marauders found our weakness, they attacked, and hundreds of my people died."

"I'm sorry." The phrase sounds paltry compared to what she has suffered. She was so young when it happened, when circumstances caused her to lose her home—her world. She'd rebuilt the physical, but I wonder at the wounds I glimpse beneath.

"What's done is done." Vera lets her arms drop to her side. "And if you really want to see that prophecy, we need to hurry."

"Why?" I ask as we swim up to the tome.

"Bacus will be back from his noon meal soon." She winks and that strange warmth spreads across my chest again. She is sneaking around for me. Somehow that endears her to me all the more.

I find myself grinning back as we thumb through the pages, looking for anything that might fit me and my situation.

"Here." Vera jabs at the section that's only four lines. All around them are drawn stars and galaxies. Two merpeople are at the bottom, hands clasped, gazing out over the endless expanse.

The words grab me, and I swallow past the bile rising in my throat.

> *There will come a foe of old*
> *Turn to merman it is foretold*
> *Then with true love he shall bind*
> *And bring about the righting of time.*

"What does it mean?" I ask, but Vera shakes her head with a shrug.

I growl, pivoting and swimming out of the library without looking back. Frustration fuels me, and I practically fly through the air as my tail flicks agitatedly. I fist my hands, wanting to hit or destroy something far too much.

I slam into someone, so lost in thought that I don't even know where I'm at.

"Watch where you're going!"

Oran.

I don't think as everything around me slows. I am mad. Whoever was fool enough to be in my way—be it King Theon himself—would have ended up as Oran did: with my hand flying toward his face.

But the Prince of Raelithion is quick, ducking away and flinging his own fist towards me. His connects with my stomach. My muffled *oomph* is followed by another growl as my mind goes on autopilot. My tail spins me around and away from Oran. As he swims closer, I feint with my left fist before swinging around with my right. I connect with his cheek, but Oran doesn't wait for an offense. His fists fly, catching my face, my chest, my arms—anywhere he can hit, he does. I manage to swing back, a few landing, but they're weak compared to Oran's.

"Enough!"

The sharp voice has us breaking apart, bleeding and gasping.

Vera rolls her eyes. "You look like a couple of children."

"He started it." Oran wipes at his bleeding lip.

Vera scoffs. "Really, Oran?"

"What?" the prince asks but Vera ignores him, swimming to my side and grabbing my arm in her frustration. "You started this? Really? What were you thinking, Ambrose?"

I gingerly brush my jaw, wincing at the pain that light touch sends shooting into my head. "I wasn't."

Vera shakes her head with a sigh. "Now that I believe. Come on, let's get you cleaned up."

"What about me?" Oran swims over, brow raised, though it looks odd with the bruising all around his eye.

"You too, hot head." Vera chuckles mirthlessly. She doesn't drop my arm, however, guiding me down the hall to our room. She orders Oran and me to sit, which we do without argument.

"I apologize, Oran. I didn't mean to start a fight," I say after Vera leaves to fetch the necessary medical supplies.

"I shouldn't have swung back." Oran rubs the back of his neck, his tail fluttering agitatedly as he drops his gaze. "I have been struggling with what to think of you, Ambrose."

"Why?" I chuckle. "I'm nothing great."

"But Bacus thinks you are. So does Father. Do you know you're the first human to pass the test?"

"The truth test?" I ask.

Oran nods. "The brand only marks those who it deems worthy, someone who is selfless in their choices." He raises his hand when I open my mouth to argue. "No one is perfect, I know. And so does the brand. It doesn't mean you'll never lie nor mess up."

"Hence your face." I can't help but smirk when Oran chuckles.

"Yes, like that. But it can see the desire of your heart. You strive to do right by others. That makes you a good man, Ambrose. And I struggle with a human being better than me."

I don't know whether to be flattered or insulted by his observation.

The door opens and Vera swims in with a tray. "I'll fix up Oran first, then treat you, Ambrose."

I nod, taking the cold pack she hands me to press against my jaw as she cleans and bandages her brother's wounds. Once she finishes, she shoos him away and Oran smiles at the door. "See you at supper?"

"Yes. Again, I'm sorry."

"It's fine. Nothing to forgive." He inclines his head before letting the door close behind him with a soft *click*.

"I've never heard him say that," Vera muses as she settles next to me to treat the cut above my eyebrow.

"Say what?"

"That an insult is *fine*." She dabs at the cut before leaning back to meet my gaze. "What happened while I was gone?"

"I think he saw that I'm no different from him."

"Aren't you?" She resumes her ministrations. "You are the one they've prophesied about."

"Are you admitting to being in love with me?" I laugh mirthlessly. "We aren't in love yet, Vera. As you've made it abundantly clear, we don't know each other."

Silence settles over the room, only broken by Vera wringing out the cloth in the warm water.

"There," she states, her voice flat. "All done."

"Thank you." I glance up, realizing how close she is. Her breath catches, her lip catching between her teeth.

Don't do it, my brain warns. *Don't even think about it.*

But all I can see is her lip caught in between her teeth.

"Vera, I want the chance to fall in love with you."

Where did those words come from? I blink.

But they're the truth. Just like my words had been true at the morning meal and the night before. I want to get to know Vera better. I want the chance to love her the way she deserves. To help her shine bright and beautiful.

Hesitantly, she cups my cheek with her hand. Some thought furrows her brow as she leans closer. "Then kiss me."

"What?" I don't pull away, but inside I jerk.

Two days, I remind myself. But, by the stars, I could kiss her senseless. I *want* to kiss her, yet I hesitate.

"Vera"—stars, my throat aches—"I would, but that wouldn't be fair to you."

"Why?" She leans closer still, her nose brushing mine now.

"Because I want to know *you*. All of you. Not just your beauty nor your kisses. I want to know your thoughts and dreams. I want to hear why you love the star fields and about your world. But if you kiss me"—I lean back, tucking a piece of hair behind her ear—"I won't be able to think about anything else."

She leans back, her expression admiring. "Oran's right then. You are a better man than him."

"You're saying your brother would have kissed you?" I tease.

Vera's mouth rounds in shock. A heartbeat passes, then she tips her head back and laughs. She lies on her back, chuckling at my bad joke as tears stream down her cheeks.

"Oh." She sits up, wiping at her cheeks. "To see Oran's face if he accidently kissed me." She giggles again, smiling up at me in my chair. Her hair is in her face. I reach down and tuck it back behind her ear.

"I mean it, Vera." I offer her my hand and we rise together. "I want the chance to fall for you."

"Try your best, Ambrose." She twines her fingers with mine, her face going solemn. "I'm already halfway there."

The next few weeks are a beautiful blur. I push the thoughts of the prophecy aside, choosing instead to learn all I can about Vera of Raelithion.

I learn that she loves the purple stars that dot the star field. The most hesitant of them all, they flock to her, scattering when I draw near.

I see her tenderness, masked as it is by the fire that courses through her veins as naturally as water flows in streams. I love when I catch glimpses of it in the spark of her eyes, in the small smiles she reserves for a choice few, or the gentle brushing of her hand against my arm or hand.

I discover that her mother was one of the people killed in the marauder raid fifteen years ago. I see the sorrow of the memories, of being brought to the palace as King Theon's illegitimate daughter. The title of princess that will never be hers. She is the whore's daughter.

The fierce desire to protect her surges in me whenever I catch the looks of disgust and hatred from those around the palace. Vera pretends to not see, but I cannot. She deserves better.

She listens as I tell her about Earth, the different places I've traveled to, both there and across the galaxies. I talk about my work with Starfleet and how much I enjoyed it. Strangely, I don't feel a desire to return. My life and heart are being drawn to Raelithion like a bug drawn to flames. I may be burned, but I no longer care.

Vera starts to show me more of her duties as a lady of the court. Though shamed by many, she has a number of jobs her father has given her. Her favorite is to help in the med bay that the palace has for those who cannot pay for medical help in the city.

The first day we journey there is two months after I was taken, and Vera swings our bound hands as she guides me to the med bay.

"Nurse Leigh is very uptight. Don't touch anything." She waits for me to nod before gliding into the infirmary.

Nurse Leigh looks up, her tight smile softening at the sight of my wife. "Oh, I am glad you're here."

Her eyes flick to me and she raises a brow. Vera smiles up at me. "He's helping me today."

"Very good." She motions to a bed in the corner. "Guard found him and brought him here. Can't get a name out of him, he seems rather delirious."

Vera nods but doesn't speak.

The nurse hands Vera heat packs. "Press these on the frost marks. He was out in space for far too long, even for a Guatople."

"A Guatople? This far into the galaxy?" Vera's brows lower and she catches her lip in her teeth, a tick I have figured out she does when she is nervous.

"What is a Guatople?" I ask as Vera takes some supplies from the nurse and motions for me to follow.

"They're…well, it's rather hard to explain." She gestures to the bed and the creature there.

My eyes widen.

"Guppy?" I grab his webbed hand, staring down at my first mate and friend. He turns his bulbous eyes toward me, a garble I can't understand slipping past his plump lips.

"You know him?" Vera sits on the other side of the bed, laying one of the packs against a grayish-blue burn on Guppy's forehead.

"He was the first mate on my starship." I swallow past the lump in my throat as Guppy closes his eyes, his gills fluttering only slightly. "What is he doing so far from earth? In space? Without a suit?"

Vera stills, her throat bobbing as she stares at my friend's green, slick skin. "Could he have been looking for you?"

"We think humans die when they're taken by the s—merpeople." I had nearly said *sirens*. "Why would he search for me?"

"Because he could know the truth, Ambrose." Her eyes flick up to me. "Before the marauders came, we kept the Guatople people as slaves."

"As *what?*" I snap, jerking up from the bed. A *shh* from Nurse Leigh has me lowering my voice. "Slaves?"

"I didn't agree with it, Ambrose, but yes. Slaves. When the marauders came, a number of the Guatoples revolted and joined them. I don't know how old your friend is, as his people age differently from us, but he might be old enough to have fought with them. Or even if he was a child, he could still remember. I do."

She had witnessed a raider slaughter her mother. Had only been saved by a courageous undercover soldier that had been guarding her. The merman had dragged her back to the palace. I thank that merman in my mind every day.

Guppy's eyes open and he stares at me. "Ambrose?"

"It's me."

"You should be dead!"

He struggles to sit up, but Vera pushes him back down. "You're not ready yet, Guppy."

"She knows my name." Guppy's skin turns a darker shade of green. "Did you tell her my name, Ambrose?"

"She's my wife, Gup."

He closes his eyes. "Oh, this is bad."

"What are you talking about?"

"Starfleet is on the border of the star cluster, Ambrose. They're readying an attack. They think the sirens have killed you." His milky brown eyes focus on me. "But you're not dead. Just…changed."

I chuckle. "I rather like my tail."

I flick it up and he turns to see it, his face paling even farther. "How come I'm not seeing you the way the siren outside the ship looked?"

I turn to Vera, who is silently watching the whole exchange.

"Because you're within our border," she supplies. "And your people were always better at seeing us less like terrors and more like creatures worthy of respect."

Guppy sighs, bubbles springing from his mouth. "Well, Ambrose better convince the Starfleet that he is fine—me too, for that matter—or war is going to come to your borders."

Vera jerks, her purple eyes landing on me with a pleading in them.

"Let's go talk to your father and brother." I rub the back of my neck. "I'll try to fix this. I don't want anything to happen to Raelithion."

"I'm more concerned about what will happen to you." She grabs my hand. Stark fear rests in her gaze. "Ambrose, if Starfleet attacks, Father could kill you for violation of the trade."

Chapter Five

We hurry down the hall, Vera's fingers threaded in mine. My heart pounds against my ribs like a jackhammer, sending aching pains across my chest.

Is this really happening? I wonder. *My two worlds are colliding. What happens if they both shatter? If I am forced to choose between Earth and Raelithion, which will I pick?*

These thoughts whirl like a vortex through my mind. I clutch onto Vera's hand like the lifeline it is even as she halts me. If we turn the corner, we will be able to see the large double doors at the end of the hall. The doors that will lead us to King Theon's throne room. They mirror the dining room doors in size, but four guards stand before it.

I have never been called before the king in my weeks here in Raelithion. The urge to trace my truth brand makes my fingers spasm.

"Ambrose," Vera whispers, drawing my gaze from the corner to her face. Her pale skin is even paler from the revelations of the day and she is chewing on her lip.

"What's wrong?"

Her eyes turn glassy, her voice cracking as she says, "I'm not ready to lose you."

"Lose me?" The absurdity of that statement snaps my spiraling thoughts out like a whip. "You're not going to lose me, Vera. The thought of going back to Earth is tempting. I lived there for twenty-five years. I have a job and parents. But Raelithion has become my home. And I fight for what I love. I'll fight for our home."

"Home? *Our* home?" Vera's mouth opens, then closes, but no words escape.

"Yes. *Our* home." I tug her closer, heat flaring through me. "This is my home. Not only Raelithion, but here. With you. Home is wherever you are."

Vera's voice is breathy when she says, "Ambrose," once more. One of her hands snakes itself around my neck, the other settles at my waist. She tugs my face closer to hers as she drinks me in. The spark in her eyes dance like the stars we love right before she presses her mouth to mine.

Heat explodes through me, hotter than a supernova. It blazes across my lips, my cheeks, down to my tail and fins. Vera deepens the kiss as I thread my fingers into her hair and kiss her back. Her tail curls around mine as she wraps her arms around my neck.

I hear something over the pounding of my heart, and though I don't want to, I ease my mouth away from my wife's. Vera's cheeks hold a pretty splash of color now and her eyes continue to dance.

"You can kiss." I could have slapped myself for the idiotic statement, except my hands are busy playing in Vera's silky pink hair.

My wife laughs. "Good. I've never done it before, so I'm glad I can."

"You've never…?" I trail off as she shakes her head, and then I chuckle in disbelief. "Well, please make me your one and only."

A throat clears and we both turn to see Oran. His face glows like the red stars in the starfield and he refuses to look at us as he states, "Father wants to see you both."

"I suppose he's heard." Vera sighs as she threads her fingers with mine.

"About what?" Oran asks as we follow him to the doors. "I can't get anything out of him."

"About the starship on the border." I wince as Oran snaps his head toward me. I have made gains with him, but I worry about what this news will do to our fragile trust.

"Yours, I presume?"

"It was my first mate in the med bay. The way he was talking means it is." I rough a hand over my face. "I don't like it anymore than you do, Oran."

"Good." King Theon's voice is hard, cold, and I fight the urge to flinch as we all turn toward him. "Because you, Ambrose, are the one who is going to convince them to leave."

"Father, that's suicide!" Vera cries. "They'll see him as a siren and destroy him."

"Perhaps." King Theon steeples his fingers, his blue tail lazily shifting in the current. "And then again, he may succeed."

"I can't lose him." Vera's voice cracks and her entire body trembles.

I wrap my arms around her, ignoring everyone else in the room. "I already said you won't."

"But they could kill you." Vera presses her face against my chest. "Then I would never get you back, Ambrose."

"The prophecy," I whisper against her hair.

She leans back to gaze at me. "What about it?"

"It says we will right a wrong. True love and all that."

"So?"

"So." I clear my throat. "I love you, Vera. Have for a while, but I needed to know that—"

Vera cuts me off as she kisses me once again. I smile against her lips, laughing in earnest as Oran makes a gagging sound.

Vera shoots her brother a look before smiling up at me. "I love you too, Ambrose. To eternity and further still."

I kiss her forehead before turning to the king once more. "I will face them. But Vera has to go with me."

King Theon opens his mouth to protest, but Oran beats him to it. "You want to take my baby sister into space? Unprotected?"

"She'll be with me, Oran." I wrap my arm around Vera's waist. "I don't want anything to happen to her either. Her safety will be top priority."

"I'm right here!" Vera tugs away. "The prophecy says that we must face it together. That both of us will right the wrong. I have to go with him, or he will die."

"We either die here together, or we risk Vera and me for the possible safety of us all." I shrug, appearing unphased even as the nerves in my stomach curl tauter with each word. "Either way, danger isn't far from us."

"If it is what needs to be done, so be it." King Theon sighs, looking much older than he had at our wedding.

With a flick of his wrist, he dismisses us. Vera and I leave, Oran on our tail.

"This is a horrible idea!" he mutters, glaring at us both. "If either of you dies, I will kill the other."

"And if both of us die?"

Oran's lips press into a thin line as he crosses his arms over his defined chest. "That better not happen."

"Rock, paper, scissors for who gets to die?" At their puzzled looks, "It's a human way to solve disagreements."

"Oh, we call it *Sun, Moon, Stars.*" Oran's face relaxes, though his muscles are still taut.

"How does that work?" I raise my brow.

"Sun is brighter than the moon, moon is brighter than the stars, and there are more stars than suns in the universe." Vera shrugs. "But that's not important."

"She's right." Oran runs a hand through his hair. "Let's get you ready to face a fleet."

I look ridiculous.

I stare down at the scaly breastplate that Vera is strapping to my chest. It's a rainbow of colors, no two the same. Oran had explained that unlike reptiles and fish on Earth, merpeople lose scales like a human loses strands of hair. The armor that they wear is made from those shed scales.

"This isn't going to stop a starship bullet," I say wryly.

"You don't know that since we never tested it. To do that, we would have had to shoot that with a Starfleet gun, something we don't have." Vera turns me to face her, strapping on metal vambraces. These, I'd been told, were made from the heart of a star. "Besides, these can."

She crosses her forearms in an X shape. I mimic her, and a bright yellow shield of energy explodes in front of me.

"Good." She places her hand over my heart. She's already outfitted in a matching breastplate and vambraces. Her hair is pulled back into a high tail, a few strands curling at her temples.

Tucking a piece behind her ear, I lean my forehead against hers. "In this together."

"Together or not at all," she agrees. "We can do this, right?"

"Let's go see." I twine my fingers with hers, leading her out of the armory and into the street of Raelithion.

They're strangely empty. The normal chatter of the merpeople is gone, replaced by an oppressive muteness that chokes me as I glide forward beside Vera. I want to gag, but the overwhelming desire to appear strong prevails.

We reach the road's end. Ahead of us stretches the endlessness of the galaxy. Trillions of stars, billions of planets, infinite possibilities. And as I stand there, with all the possible futures it holds waiting at my fingertips, there is only one for me. She's clutching my hand, still afraid I will let her go.

"I'm scared," Vera says.

"Me too," I admit. "But if I'm going to face it, there's no one I'd rather do it with than you."

"Do you think they'll shoot at us?" She shivers.

I tug her closer, our scaly armor making a grating noise. "Maybe."

We stand like that for another long moment before I sigh and tug her off the road, and into the empty space beyond.

It is a strange sensation, gliding over nothing. It dwarfs me, showing me how easily it could be for me to snuffed out. And the silence. It crushes me worse than the quiet of the street had moments before.

Coldness seeps around us as the light from the stars nearest Raelithion fades the farther we swim. Gooseflesh springs across my arms and I wish for the warmth those scant stars provide. My mind conjures the images of Guppy's dead flesh and bile burns my throat.

Vera doesn't let go of my hand as we approach the starship. The large glass window of the cockpit and command center gleam in the starlight, and I can see the people inside bustling to and fro. How often had I stood there on the bridge, ordering them about? Did I miss it?

No, my mind immediately supplies. *You did it because you had to. But you never enjoyed it.*

I adjust my grip on Vera's hand as we glide up to the window. All the motion inside ceases, every eye turning toward us with open-mouthed shock.

I don't recognize the man on the bridge. He's older, with gray at his temples. His eyes narrow as he points toward us, his bushy mustache twitching as he orders something.

A trembling cadet steps to the window, his words barely audible. "What do you want?

"I am Ambrose of Earth."

Everyone I can see startles, glancing at the man on the bridge. His eyes are large, mini moons in his tan face.

"How are you a siren?" the cadet asks, shaking harder. "What witchcraft is this?"

"It's no witchcraft," I protest. "I traded myself for the safety of my crew."

"Who is that with you?"

Vera swims around me and chaos ensues. Guns and shields are raised around the ship, forcing us to swim away from the window. I push Vera behind me as I try to shout through the chaos of the humming and clanking and hissing.

"We're going to die." Vera whimpers and protectiveness flares in me.

"No, we're not." I turn, gripping her face in my hands. "I didn't choose to marry you. I chose to save my crew, that's all. But now, I won't let you go. I'm in love with you, Vera. Madly, completely in love. Raelithion is my home."

Heat flares in me and I tug her closer, my tail curling around hers. I soak her in. Her purple eyes, her hair that's floating around her weightlessly, her pale skin that glows in the light of the shield.

"If the worst happens, it happens together," I vow.

She leans her forehead against mine. The humming increases, they're going to shoot us at any moment. My breathing grows ragged, my muscles tense. I lean in closer, my lips brushing Vera's in a feather light kiss. She leans against me, and I taste tears as I leave a smattering of kisses across her cheekbones.

The humming fades as our fervor grows. The cold scatters like a glass shattering against a stone floor. *Vera.* Her name swells in me like an ocean wave, growing in size that it could swallow kingdoms. I could go anywhere, be anything, *do* anything if I have her working and loving and living beside me.

I pull away, grabbing her wrist. I eye the vambrace and smile coyly.

"What are you doing?" she asks as I turn back to the ship.

All the guns are trained on us, whirring loudly in the vacuum of space. I throw back my shoulders. "I am Ambrose of Earth and this is the kingdom of Raelithion! It is under my protection, and you shall not harm *anyone* here or suffer my wrath!"

The man on the bridge is laughing, I can tell. I lock my jaw, crossing my wrist with Vera's. The click of metal is muted as an explosion of light shoots out of our crossed arms. It snakes to the ship, taking out every gun as it leaps from side to side.

Vera gasps, her free hand finding mine. We stand as a wall of protection for our people. A few spattering blasts try to hit us, but they fizz out before they reach past the shield.

"Stronger together," I whisper.

We drop our arms once the guns are eradicated. Everyone inside the ship is on their knees. The man with the mustache is the only one standing. He walks to the window, a begrudging respect in his large-eyed gaze.

"What are your orders, Master Ambrose?" he asks.

"Leave Raelithion and never return." I straighten. "If you wish to return under the banner of peace, we may consider a trade deal. But only maybe. I speak for the Raelithions. They deserve to be heard in this galaxy. They are not the monsters that we feared. They are so much more."

The man smiles slightly, eying Vera. "Perhaps you are the bridge to mend this gap in human knowledge."

"If something is imperfect, it needs work," Vera whispers, meeting the captain's gaze. "Work takes time, sir. Is that something the humans are willing to give?"

"Possibly." His brow raises and I'm surprised he can understand Vera, being fully mermaid as she is. The captain smiles at my wife. "But then, they're a stubborn lot."

"Teach them, Captain." I incline my head. "And until they understand, keep them away from Raelithion."

He nods.

"First Mate Guppy shall remain with us. Now, you're free to go."

He nods again before barking orders to the crew. The ship hums to life, turning slowly around and gliding away from our home. We watch as they hit the lightleap and disappear in a blast of light.

Vera shivers violently and I wrap my arms around her.

"Let's go home," I whisper into her hair and she nods without a protest.

When our tails brush the brick walkways, merfolk pour from their homes, cheering and celebrating us. But I cannot celebrate. Vera leans heavily against me, her body shaking from the toll of our swim in space. I push through the people, reaching our room and laying her onto the bed. I brush her hair from her forehead and she smiles up at me.

"We did it," she mumbles, cradling my hand to her cheek.

I nod, my throat feeling thick as I whisper, "Yes, we did."

"Stay with me, Ambrose."

"Always."

I tug the blankets over us, feeling a wave of exhaustion slam into me. I cradle Vera as my eyes slip closed. We had protected Raelithion. We had fulfilled the prophecy. Now was the time to rest.

Guppy

Prince Oran is the one to find them, cold and lifeless among their blankets. The doctors say they expended too much energy when they joined their vambraces. In saving Raelithion, they destroyed themselves.

I—Guppy, formerly of Earth, now of Raelithion—am given the task of saying a speech on their behalf. I weep during most of it. How does one pay tribute to a man who gave so much? A woman who I met only once? Yet I had seen the love in my friend's gaze for his wife. He treasured her. His sacrifice had gained him so much. And in a single breath it had all been snuffed out.

I stand now in a starfield. The light of these tiny balls of fire seems dimmer than normal. I reach out, cupping a red spark in my palm. It pulses faintly and I want to weep with it. I have been told they spent much time here, Ambrose and Vera. Even the stars mourn them.

"Are you all right, friend?"

I turn to see Oran leaning against a pillar to the doorway. His eyes are sad, his tail listlessly swaying in the space current.

"No."

He smiles sadly. "They knew the risk. It was one they were both willing to make. They brought peace."

"At what cost?" I choke on a breath, my gills closing for an infinitely long time. "At what cost, my prince?"

"They loved, Guppy." The merman swims forward. "They loved and were loved and sacrificed for love. I can think of few more noble goals, few worth that cost."

"For the love of their people, they gave themselves up?"

"Aye." Oran smiled, more sadness creeping up and spilling out his eyes. "And while I miss them dreadfully, I cannot wish them back."

He tips his head back, surveying the sky above us. "They swim now in the heavens. The stars will bless them in their journey."

"How do you know?"

Oran's smile grows, and this time, it contains a hope I cannot feel. "Because I can hear them, my friend. Their song is in the stars. Can't you hear it?"

I tip my head to the side, listening. At first, nothing happens. The eerie silence wraps around me like a damp blanket. I want nothing more than to shove it off.

But then, softly, like the breath of a kiss on the cheek, a song swirls around me. It hums of peace, of a journey beyond. The stars brighten, dancing through the garden on the waves of the hopeful tune. Around me they fly, faster and faster. My heart matches the tempo, my chest aching at the sheer beauty of it. A crescendo of joy rises and then slows and softens, humming of hope anew.

"They're in a better place." Oran promises, clasping my shoulder. "They will always be with us, journeying with us among the stars."

"Aye." I sigh. "But I shall miss them."

Oran nods. "Then let us live like they did. Let us see the beauty around us, fix what is wrong with our world, and never stop fighting for love."

As we move toward the doorway, I glance over my shoulder one last time. The stars have formed a picture, hovering in the black sky. Ambrose's face smiles at me and he winks before the stars break the image into a shower of dancing lights.

"I'll keep fighting, my friend." I fist my hand over my heart. "I'll keep fighting."

BLUE IN THE DEEP

Catherine Kopf

"So here you are: too foreign for home, too foreign for here. Never enough for both."

\-
                                        Ijeoma Umebinyuo

Entry 01—Planet H0M3, Creature Research Journal:

15:00 hours. I'm worried about how my husband is raising my son, Coral. We watched a movie last night, where the new was frightening and all the creatures dangerous. My husband says BLUE *will be a good place for him, and I know Coral picked to live with him on the extraordinary submarine, but there are no children like Coral on* BLUE. *It rams into the rocks and ecosystems here, destroying all in its path to use a substance clinging onto rocks and cliffs for fuel. Creatures need every piece of their ecosystem to keep natural order. There are a variety of creatures that use this substance, but it looks like coral from home. I've decided to label it as* kōraru, *after the creature my husband and I loved to look at in cerulean waters on Earth.*

I'm hoping this journal will create an environment of love and compassion for the creatures here, so we do not use the resources in the wrong way and ruin what we have here on H0M3. May we

*learn from our mistakes and not stay ignorant of the environmental
damage that destroyed our old home.*
-                          *Dr. Judith Langhostin*

They say seventy-one percent of Earth is covered by
water, but this sea stretches on forever. Far out into the
horizon, a blurred line of water meets the sun and melds
colors into a peaceful pinkish-purple. Orange kelp sticks
out of the ocean and waves in the breeze. Below it,
mounds of neon-green and fluorescent-blue coral look
like glow-in-the-dark sponges stuck in an overfilled
kitchen sink.

I kick my leg in the water, hitting BLUE when
returning to my criss-cross position. The submarine
clunks as my boot's rubber heel nicks the metal that's
quickly fading from blue to a metallic silver. BLUE looks
like a shark, though he's way bigger—big enough to fit a
city's worth of people. With his square-ish shaped head,
headlamp eyes, and flippers that help us balance, his tail
is the motor to help us explore ocean depths. But BLUE
isn't just an item; BLUE is home now.

I move my feet again, causing a ripple large enough
to expose even more of the orange and pink coral
glowing underneath. I smile. *More coral. Guess Dad's right, I
do attract coral. No wonder it's my name.* In my diving gear, I
could conquer the ocean and explore it to my heart's
content, but that's more of Mom's job on the landbase.
I'm just along for the ride on BLUE with Dad and a few

other kids—kids that know nothing about swimming or Earth's sea life. Most don't even know ocean facts like me…or my mom before the Split.

I lower my head to gaze into the water and the coral below me. Something as big as me swiftly swishes by, flickering a whale-like tail. I jump and my heart races. Is it a shark? A dolphin? By the size, it can't be a whale.

It passes by again, and this time I get a glimpse of the creature's bright colors among the neon coral.

It swims toward the surface, staring at me with sideways-blinking eyes as it swirls around my feet.

I adjust my thin, round glasses to see its cat-like pupils better.

What are you?

It has the head of a snake, but no fangs as it opens its mouth, only gums to chew up pudding if it wanted. Large round eyes—like a sea lion—stare at me, and two tentacles touch my hand. Looking into the water, a neon-green glow shines from scales reflecting off the light. It has a whale's tail, which rocks up and down, unlike BLUE's side to side motion, and six spines like a pufferfish for hair. But its torso doesn't remind me of sea creatures; it looks like a human's…like me. I place my hand on my chest and lean in to get a better look at what—who—I'd found.

I wave my hand at it and it waves its hand back like a reflection. I tilt my head, it does the same. As I blink, it matches my moments again. I take out a notebook from my jacket pocket and jot down notes.

Why match my movements? Just curious? Or does it need something?

As I'm writing, the creature reaches its tentacle hand out of the water and grabs my glasses off my face. In the deep, it inspects them like a toddler with a new toy, checking every angle and even putting them on before handing them back. Slime oozes off the frames.

Definitely curious. I jot down my discovery and try to make a quick sketch. *Dad is going to be so stoked! If only Mom could—*

I put down my pencil and sigh. The creature hugs my legs and pulls me into the water. It catches me by surprise. I flap my arms as I bob up to the surface and back down again with the creature still grabbing my legs. I struggle for air before it lets me go. Its lip is pouting as I cough up the salty water. Water's still dripping from the cover's surface of my notebook, ruined by the water. It's okay though, I have a few left.

You're not used to seeing humans, huh?

The creature swims below and breaks off a piece of orange coral, putting it next to me as I climb onto BLUE's fin. I grab the rough chunk of coral and smile. Maybe it isn't so bad.

I feel bad for calling him "it"—maybe I should give him a name? I'm guessing it's a boy. I take out my blue compass and give it to him. A smile forms on its face. *Compass. I guess it fits. It goes well with Coral, so why not?*

Compass is mesmerized with the way the compass reacts to movement. The device remembers north based on the planet's magnetic poles, but I'm guessing he doesn't know that. Instead, he turns in all directions while holding the device in his tentacles, flipping about the coral reef and purple kelp stretching above the water.

He gets back to me before his eyes go wide and he swims away, the compass still firm in his grasp.

My dad taps my shoulder and signs to me in ASL. "Let's get down below."

I close my notebook and nod. Dinner's getting close anyway.

Entry 26—Planet H0M3, Creature Research Journal:

19:00 hours. DEEP sea exploration has led me to a species of humanoid sea life here on H0M3. The species cannot speak English, but it mimics my movements and sounds. Coral would've loved to meet them. When I repeated his name aloud, they said "Kor-al", trying to grasp how my language works. On further examination, they communicate mainly through hand movements, like sign language. I'll keep a record of our new friends. We're invading their habitat with things like BLUE, and our best course of action is to learn from them, as curious as they may be. I named the small creature I encountered today, Alpha.

22:00 hours. Alpha and a few others have followed me back to the lab and show an interest in the coral collection. They are not bothered much by other organisms in their ecosystem, and seem to be social creatures. Their lack of teeth makes them likely to be herbivores; perhaps coral is their food source? I'll have to check its sustainability.

Dr. Judith Langhostin

"I want to visit home," I sign to my dad from where I lie in bed. I bite my lip. *When would we be there again?*

He signs back with a smile. "We are on Home."

"Not that Home. Our home." I point to the picture on the dresser of Dad, Mom, and me at a Dodgers game when I was five or six. Dad said he caught a ball and handed it over to me before kissing Mom while a photographer took our picture. It hasn't been the same since Earth died and BLUE became part of my dad's job.

Dad taps my shoulder and shakes his head, as if he guesses there is a lot on my mind. He signs, "This is Home now, champ. Maybe we can watch a movie tomorrow with some school friends of yours?"

I clasp my hands together and exhale deeply. *Friends? What friends? No one at school can sign. The teacher has to use captions and writing for me. They don't want to go through all the effort. It's like trying to hug a pufferfish! Except Compass today…* I sign back, "I think I made a new friend today actually, but he won't be able to come tomorrow."

Dad tucks me into bed, chuckling at my sea turtle pajamas. He ruffles my hair and smiles. "Well, there you go, Coral! Hang out with your friend more and try to get over this sea stuff. There's a lot of innovation and exploration to do in BLUE too."

I pout as he turns off the light, but as the whale and shark mobile spins around the room above my head, it reminds me why I chose Dad in the first place: BLUE is supposed to be exciting but comfortable, where I could make tons of friends like back on Earth.

Yet I still remember how Mom kissed me when tucking me into bed at her house. The cookies warm enough to lull me to sleep themselves, the tales of when she and dad traveled together to learn more about sea life before BLUE. Before we lost Earth… Before they…

I clutch my covers tightly. A red light blinks in the corner of the room. My room is so small and cold here, it's like an ice cream container. BLUE rocks a lot, especially by the airplane-like fins and tail where its engines are. My room is right outside the left fin, and the rocking makes my stomach swirl like a whirlpool. Mom's house never made me sick, but it didn't have a window looking out into the ocean either.

Gazing out through the small, circular porthole, I get a glimpse of the sea life, glowing in the deep as they pass each other. Some look like speckled dolphins, others are hybrids of seahorses and cuttlefish—spiny but cute. Half-crab, half squid creatures cling onto the fin of BLUE, letting their tentacles grasp onto it and their hard shells protect their heads from other creatures coming BLUE's way.

Compass is out there too, flipping his tail to move in circles with the compass I gave him. Still trying to figure out how it works, I guess.

I press my hand against the window before grabbing the piece of coral and my notebook from my desk. Sitting crisscross-applesauce, I finish my sketch of Compass, watching him smile and flip around before settling on BLUE's fin with the squabs—that's a fitting name for the squid-crabs, right?

Compass curls into a ball by my window and falls fast asleep. I slump over and sigh, rubbing the orange coral, now glowing in the dark. *What is he still doing here?*

"Some creatures are too curious for their own good, Coral, including people." Mom's words echo in my head as I recall her brushing through my hair the night before she left BLUE. *"I still love you. You know that, right? Even though you chose Dad, this home is still yours when you want it."*

Knots form in my stomach as I head back into bed.

Entry 27—Planet HOM3, Creature Research Journal:

7:00 hours. The kōraru eaten by Alpha and his species has specific properties, some more rare than others. For example, the kōraru lights up at night due to storing solar energy. Even with three moons, HOM3 is pitch-black in the deepest parts of its ocean. But these creatures take kōrarus when exploring into those regions and even in their cave habitats. Orange kōraru is the least eaten by the group, preferring to use it near underwater volcanoes and hot springs to carry heat. Blue kōraru is the most common food source. There's so much of it on the planet, and they always try to take only what they need. Humans—we could've done better back on Earth before the climate and resource crisis. BLUE is going to put us back in the same situation.

14:00 hours. Alpha is starting to understand sign language and English as he teaches me about his writing and signing system. He comes from an intelligent species like ours, with ink made from their squid-like tentacles. They have thirty symbols for an alphabet, including whole characters to produce various sounds. Coral, or

"Kor-Al", for instance, has three letters, one for "ck," one for "or" and one for "al". Seeing these creatures wanting to teach me about their worldview reminds me of how much I miss teaching my son. We're oceans apart on a planet filled to the brim with the sea life we love.

-                    *Dr. Judith Langhostin*

Do I remember the day I boarded BLUE for the first time?

I replay the events in my head.

I held hands with Mom and Dad as we entered BLUE from its rear, a place where small submarines could move in and out of the city of BLUE. We'd just exited our family submarine, and my parents pointed at the sign at the top of the opening. "WELCOME TO HUMANITY'S FIRST BIOLOGICAL LOGISTICAL UNDERWATER ECOSYSTEM ON H0M3. LET OUR CITY BE YOUR NEW HOME!" And that's what BLUE was. While being an intimidating shark on the outside, larger than any whale back on Earth and able to fit in the depths, inside it was a spitting image of my home back in California. At least that's what Dad said he designed it after.

Kids scurried about on the playground in front of me; some dribbled basketballs while others climbed monkey bars and slid down slides. They smiled and pointed at each other. Some hugged and looked my way, moving their mouths, but I couldn't hear a sound.

Mom signed for me. *"They're wondering why you're not playing, Coral."*

Her mouth moved as she said something to Dad. He shook his head and knelt down to look me in the eye. Mom pinched the bridge of her nose.

"Go play with them." Dad smiled and signed fast. I almost didn't catch it.

A girl my age with curly blonde hair approached me. She moved her mouth, but again, I stood with a blank stare. *I can't understand her.* The girl waved awkwardly, her smile turning sour like she'd bitten into a lemon as she walked off.

I stared at the holographic screen of the Golden Gate Bridge flickering in and out as Dad's tape looped. Dodger Stadium seemed too far away. Fake grass tickled my toes, but it wasn't the same. It smelled like plastic; it was too rough to be real. I was alone in a big sea, with only Mom and Dad to comfort me.

I gripped their hands tighter as we made our way through the crowds of people, like fish among coral flocking together to be safer.

It was night time when we first made it to our complex on BLUE. I still remember the metallic smell from the walls as we first walked through the door. Dad held a movie in his hand, THE DEEP, which he signed was an alien-science-fiction movie with scenes actually filmed underwater before the ocean on Earth got too polluted.

I can't remember going into the ocean on Earth. By the time I was old enough to swim and remember it, the pollution had gotten too bad. Movies with Earth's ocean always interested me, but aliens? Weren't we the aliens on H0M3? I could do with less aliens in my life.

Mom and Dad sat on either side of me on the couch as the film started. Bubbles surfaced, kelp and sea life emerging as the camera headed into the water. Fish swarmed in clusters as they scurried away from something coming closer in the water. Each fish shimmered as the camera whisked past it. It wasn't one of those CGI films made after the pollution. The bubbles, the fish, their movements, it was all real.

Dad tapped my shoulder. "Oooh! The alien sure got him, didn't it buddy?"

What? The alien was there? Was I supposed to notice that?

Mom knocked my dad's shoulder with her arm, moving her mouth to make words I couldn't hear. Dad's brow furrowed as he opened his mouth wide. I gazed back and forth at my parents, feeling like I was watching fish open their mouths from inside an aquarium tank, only these fish were angry, like predators about to get into a fight.

I just focused on the outside window of BLUE, with squabs and other unique creatures. I couldn't finish the movie.

Neither could Mom.

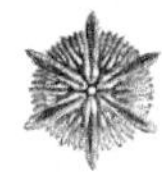

I shiver this flashback away and adjust my swimming goggles. A few more days have passed since I met Compass, but he seems just as bold and curious as ever.

We swim back and forth on the surface and collect coral after coral—one in each color so Compass could see colors like me. I smile at my collection in the bag beside me. We've found ways to communicate through body language and observing each other. He smiles when he's happy and his tail moves faster than normal too, like a dog's. Compass occasionally invites me deeper to pet a squab or a sea-elephant or two, but I never go under or beyond BLUE's fins.

BLUE is the only one from Earth who gets to constantly be in the deep. It isn't that the water on Home is toxic; it just goes on and on for miles. When Mom and Dad split, she stayed on the only man-made land base studying creatures and Dad chose to work as an engineer on BLUE.

I place my bare feet into the cold water and let the sea elephants wrap their small trunks around my toes. It tickles as they rub back and forth and suck on my feet. Occasionally, I have to shake them off when there's too many. Dad compares them to leeches whenever he's around, which isn't often thanks to his job to keep BLUE running. They don't suck blood like leeches though. They don't even have teeth to bite into my skin. That's what Mom says.

"Mom, where is home? Is it on Home?" I remember the first time we found sea-elephants, she scooped some into a jar and placed them like goldfish in an aquarium.

She sighs and adjusts the jar before signing back. *"Home is a feeling, not a place. Even if we aren't on Earth anymore, anywhere can be home if it's with the things and people you love."*

Is BLUE really home? I thought it could be a place where I would make friends and explore while still feeling at home. Now, part of me wants to sink into the deep and let it lead me where it wants me to go. I could talk with Compass, the squabs, and maybe find my mother researching new creatures along the way. We'd climb the kelp and plant some in the garden; she'd make me cookies and shape them like dolphins, whales, and sharks as we talk about the new adventures we'd find. But the other part of me wants to stay grounded and learn about the depths from the safety of BLUE. My stomach churns; it's like I've eaten too much ice cream, only…I haven't done that.

What's really home when it's two places at once? I swallow hard and clench my toes in the water, scaring off some of the sea elephants. My two homes seem too far apart for me to touch both, a vast ocean between them.

Entry 28—Planet H0M3, Creature Research Journal:

5:00 hours. I've finally tried the pink coral upon Alpha's insistence. "Eaat." He kept repeating it over and over, biting on the coral after telling me this. Several instances went by where I considered it, but I actually took the plunge today. I tried pink coral and dove into the deep without my diving gear. After studying these creatures on H0M3, I've learned just how adaptive they can be when learning about things and other creatures surrounding them. One even gave me a blue compass, an item I recognize as the one I gave Coral the day before I left BLUE.

As I've researched and studied about this planet, I've learned a few things. A being similar to humanity evolved to survive here. Humanity has to do the same. We can't keep living how we lived on Earth. We don't even have Earth anymore, yet, so many people keep blinders up and pretend that BLUE is a "New Earth". It's not; it tears objects out of its way, it simulates a planet that's dead rather than embrace the new Home around us. We don't need to use the resources to the point of extinction. We need to understand them.

7:00 hours. This will be my final entry. I've decided to move out of the land base and into a place where I feel more at home. If Coral wants to join me in my explorations, he can. I've never shut my doors.

Signing off. May humanity learn from its mistakes.
-
　　　　　　Dr. Judith Langhostin

Compass flips about in the water to get my attention, waving about before diving below. I lean forward and he does it again.

He wants me to go under again. He knows I can't breathe there, so what's up?

Under the water, he bites a piece of luminescent pink coral, and it squishes in his mouth as his jaw clamps down. But above water, it's as hard as a rock. *Without teeth, how can Compass...?*

I lower my piece into the water, the substance softening in my hand. *It's squishy in water.* Compass continues to eat his piece and flips again, his signal for me to get into the water. *He wants me to eat it in the water too. Why? Can I even trust Compass? He's lost out—*

I can't finish that thought. It isn't even true. He's more at home than I am here on Home. Sea elephants swim around my legs, kelp grows higher than the water line and the pinkish-purple horizon reflects off the deep's water. I feel like I'm sitting alone at the school lunch tables back on Earth, only the people are much further away. It's just me, Compass, and the open sea.

I'm tapped on the shoulder and turn right. Mom's standing behind me, her smile the same as mine. She's different from before, with webbed hands and feet. Slits in her neck show off gills. Her hair is like kelp. Still, she's here. She's come to see me.

Tears run down her face as her webbed hands embrace me. When we release, she holds out the blue compass—the same one I gave Compass that fateful day. Warm fuzziness fills me up from my head to my toes as I grip the object, taking it from her as she brushes through my hair.

Mom signs. "Coral. It's so nice to see you!"

"Mom, you're like them now! How?"

"The pink coral." Mom smiles. "I chose to explore the deep and become part of this planet. How are you doing?"

"I made friends with Compass, but…"

"But?"

"Home is a feeling, not a place. Even if we aren't on Earth anymore, anywhere can be home if it's with things and people you love." Mom's words echo into my head again.

I sign with confidence. "BLUE doesn't feel like home, even if it is in the deep."

"Then do you want to come with Compass and me and explore together?" Mom holds out a piece of the pink coral. "We can help the planet instead of hurting it."

I nod, eager to be with the nature I love so much.

Mom jumps back into the water with a splash. Slipping into the water with my piece of coral, I take a breath. Compass is popping above the surface before diving into the deep again, wanting me to copy the motion and eat the coral.

Dad runs onto the deck and leans over, looking at me in the water with widened eyes. He signs frantically. "Get below. Now. What are you doing with these monsters?"

"They aren't monsters!" I look at my friend, cowering behind me and Mom swimming beside me.

"They're aliens—that makes them dangerous." Dad shoos them away with his hands and grabs his communicator to alert the crew, but stops when he recognizes Mom. He speaks up and scrunches his face, confused by her statement, but I can only see his mouth move.

Mom signs, the corners of her mouth frowning. "We're the aliens here! If Coral wants to explore The Deep, we need to do it in a natural way. He's alone on BLUE."

"BLUE is your home now." Dad's brow furrows as Compass opens his mouth—I can't hear the noise, but by Dad's face, it's horrifying. "Come inside. You'll end up just as alone as your mother out there."

I clutch the coral in my hands before putting it back under my arm to sign, "I already feel that way on BLUE."

Dad pauses, no signs, no talking to Mom, not even a gesture. His face is blank for a few moments before he reaches out to the water. "Coral, I'm sorry. Things can get better here, if you want. But do you really want to go explore that much?"

I nod and come closer to hold his hand.

He sighs, I can see it in his slumping shoulders, and puts on a smile for me. "But you have to promise to visit, okay?"

"Really Dad? You mean it?"

Dad nods and brushes my fingers. "I think it's time you see BLUE from the deep."

Dad grabs his scuba gear and comes with me into the water. Mom hands me the piece of pink coral and Dad nods. Compass swishes around with excitement.

I'm really doing this. Here goes nothing!

I take a bite of the squishy coral. At first, the world spins and my heart beats hard to keep up with the adrenaline I have inside. My hands and feet ache, my head pounds. *This is a mistake! I have to get up!* I struggle to catch my breath and can't seem to find my way to the surface. *This is it.*

Mom hugs me; Dad does the same. They're still here to help me as I work through this. I smile despite how I feel on the outside. *I can tackle anything with them.*

The feelings of pain soften; my muscles relax with a wash of the ocean currents flowing around me like air.

And I take a breath underwater with newly formed gills on my neck.

I feel the opening flaps as they extend in and out. Compass is whirling around me, letting me see a glimpse of BLUE's full body for the first time. My feet and hands are webbed like a frog's, and I move like the ocean is nothing to tread across. It's like a hike where you float, a walk in a coral and kelp park.

"What do you think, champ?" Dad asks, bubbles coming from his oxygen mask. "This is BLUE from top to bottom."

BLUE really is a large shark: the submarine has a tail that sways side to side and fins that extend out, a top fin that catches attention on the surface, and front teeth to crush obstacles. It keeps secret people inside, who I see in the windows pretending they're still on Earth like nothing happened. They're still shopping and eating family dinners; they're playing with friends in rooms or drawing pictures of Earth.

But in the deep, BLUE could be seen for what it really is: a place for people not ready to accept Home as our new home.

The kelp dances in the water, wiggling as BLUE slowly passes by. Compass swirls around them and enters the entryway of an underwater cave, decorated with coral at the front to light it in a welcoming glow. Mom takes my hand and leads me inside as I wave goodbye to Dad.

As I enter, several Compasses surround me, each with different colors and sizes. They embrace Compass and wave me onward, deeper into the cavern with Mom. Structures carved from rock and decorated with kelp and coral lay beneath here, houses with lights shining inside like home, only more connected through passageways. It's like an ant farm with gray cave walls instead of dirt, water instead of air, and lights shining to guide the way to each house. The creatures have their own stores and gardens, restaurants and houses, and even places like parks. Some people look like Mom and me too, with webbed hands and feet in these places too. There are even a few kids there with their parents, smiling and playing in the deep.

Mom leads me to a house near the center of the cave system, where a sign waits reading "Kor-al". Compass opens the door with a smile and pushes me inside.

I knock against the cave wall, hoping someone can hear it nearby. I enter the house further, finding an aquarium of sea elephants and the familiar scent of cookies, only now they're made of coral.

Mom puts her forehead against mine and signs. "Welcome Home, Coral. Welcome to our place in The Deep."

THE SERAPHIC ITEM

K. Weikel

Chills race down my spine as a pocket of cold water passes. Flicks of tails echo to my otoliths, telling me the fish are close. The vibrations in the water tell me all I need to know; I don't even need to use my other sensory tools.

My spear pierces a passing fish, and by the shape and feel, I'd say it's a small shark. Maybe a blacktip.

"This will be fine for a day," I mumble to myself as I kick my tail and turn the other direction. The device on my wrist sends tiny electric pulses through my body, telling me I'm headed in the right direction. The location is always zeroed in on home, since I was told I tend to wander too far. I'd once had a…friend that tinkered. He created a few things with me to help with my handicap.

And then he disappeared.

As I near my home, the pulses increase. The familiar scents lift to my nares and puts my brain at ease. I find myself growing nervous sometimes on my journeys since I have no one to come with me any longer, but my senses surpass any other mermaid's. I believe it's the reason I was…removed from the community.

The familiar scent of home fills my pores and I smile, but I don't let my guard down. There aren't many surface bipeds that come this far out, but there's always a possibility. My friend used to warn me about them. We seemed to meet in strange ways, almost always in a curious or helpful nature. Before the community exiled me, I heard rumors of humans greeting us with violence in order to take our treasures. It's entirely possible. We're a lot weaker than sea dragons.

The device on my wrist pulses twice, letting me know I've arrived, but my nerves alight as I touch the entryway. The sea flowers that had once been there are crushed, their perfumes saddened with death's heaviness. My fingers tighten around my spear. Have the surface dwellers found my home, coming like the enemy to kill, steal, and destroy? Or worse… Did they touch the Item?

Quietly, I slip through the tattered seaweed covering the entryway, listening for any noise at all.

Labored breathing, water ripping in and out of gills deeper within.

I creep forward, forcing my gills to filter quietly as I abandon the shark I'd caught, hearing it drift to the floor. It's long been dead, and if I make it out of this alive, it'll be on a path to my digestion tract.

I draw closer to the breathing, using the walls to guide me. Worn out knots tell me which direction I'm going, what area I'm drifting toward, but it's been a long time since I've needed them as a crutch.

Spear ready, I yank aside the seaweed leading to my sleeping room, and bare my teeth. "State your business."

"Anamara!"

That voice. Why didn't I recognize his scent?

"Anamara, it's me. I'm…sorry, I didn't know where else to go."

"Toru," I breathe, dropping my spear and rushing over. My hands touch his shoulder, at which he grunts, pulling away. I don't sense blood. "Where are you hurt?"

He gives a sardonic laugh. "Is everywhere an answer you'll accept?"

"What happened? Who did this to you?"

I can't stop thinking about how long he's been gone, how lonely I've been without him. Why has he come back? Did he bring who attacked him along? There are so many trinkets he's made that have stopped working and need repairs. I didn't ever think they'd work again. Even the device around my wrist will stop working in the future, and I'll have to think of other ways to find my home.

"They followed me," he answers, pain in every sound he makes. "I've stopped the blood—raided your supplies. Apologies."

I hesitate, still not sensing any blood. His body gives off that yes, he's hurt, but nothing fatal.

"Who followed you?" I pry, his hands pushing mine away. "Are we in immediate danger?"

"I'm stabilized," Toru admits, his tone filled with guilt. "But, Anamara, they took it."

My blood turns to ice as I stop moving. "They… Who's they?"

"I couldn't stop them," he breathes. "The village is dying. We've been attacked three times in the past two years. We need it back so the Guardians can protect us."

Slowly, I rise from the ground, vibrations in the water around me. There are others here, others I hadn't realized were there. They were perfectly still as I was distracted, my emotions heightened for a dear friend.

Or someone I thought was one.

Panic clogs my throat. The prophecy… "Toru… Please tell me you didn't."

Toru hesitates as I sense him rising. "I'm sorry."

Something crashes against the back of my head, knocking me out cold.

I wake with pounding in my skull. My wrists are bound, and a weight around the end of my tail keeps me stationary. I stay still and keep my eyelids shut, straining with all my might to assess my surroundings.

Movement before me, two people talking to one another in hushed tones. I hate to say I recognize them.

"Kamins, Jaksul," I mutter to the two Guardians, opening my eyes. "Always a pleasure to be in your presence."

"She's awake," Kamins announces.

"About time," Jaksul mutters. He drifts closer. "Took you long enough to wake up."

"You've returned the item to our village, I assume." I grind my teeth, trying to keep a smile on my face. "Even after my warnings."

"It isn't your village anymore. You're the reason we went searching for the Item in the first place."

I hum a laugh. "And so you blackmailed my only friend."

"They didn't blackmail me." Toru's voice echoes to my ears. It seems I'm in some sort of chamber, where the currents can't reach. The water is stagnant and rank in my mouth.

Or perhaps it's the two Guardians and the traitor putting a bad taste in it.

"Paid you, then?" I guess, snapping my head in his direction. Keeping the smile on my face, I speak slowly to work out the spikes in my nerves. "I should have known you'd betray me. Merpeople like me can never have real friends."

"Anamara, I—"

"That's enough, Toru." The voice of our village leader dredges a lick of anger from within my chest. "Jaksul, Kamins, don't keep the other Guardians waiting. The enemy is approaching."

"Narsana," I grind. "How lucky am I to attend a party led by those that stabbed my back and twisted the blade?"

Silence greets me as she approaches, the Guardians exiting. She stops directly in front of me, pausing like she doesn't know what she's about to say, but she's always been cool and calculated. She knows the reaction and answer to everything she'll say or ask. If she doesn't, she says nothing.

"You brought death upon our people after being exiled. We agreed on your punishment long ago, but you took our protection and cloaked your whereabouts."

I chuckle. "How narcissistic of you to believe you're the hero in the story. I warned about the death and ruin, and you only laughed in my face. You would have followed my mother to the grave if she were here. Her blessing was bestowed on me, and yet you spat in my face."

Pain spreads across my cheek as she strikes me.

"Your mother was a genuine Oracle. How dare you claim to have her gift when it's you who killed her."

I grit my teeth. No one listens when I tell them it was an accident, that I was scared for my life. They weren't there when my mother's mind was destroyed by demons.

Open your mind too far and madness will take you. That's what she would tell me. She was a remarkable mother, making sure I knew between right and wrong, and when to stand for something, and when to back down to fight another day. She taught me to always do what I believed was right, even if it ruffled feathers—even if she didn't have the guts to do what needed to be done herself.

"The devastation would have been catastrophic for everyone we know—"

"Nothing would have happened if you didn't steal the Item." Narsana pauses. We've been through this before, but she never takes what I say to heart. "An Oracle cannot be blind. You wouldn't even know what you're being shown."

"Sight isn't the only form of seeing," I snap, my pulse thrumming in my ears. "God uses all things for good, does He not? And didn't He make me both a Guardian and an Oracle?"

"If you think you're hearing God, you should pray," Narsana tells me, getting closer to my face. "Why would He ever use someone as filthy as you?"

Watch your words, my mother would tell me. *Death and life are in the tongue, never forget that.*

Narsana shifts. I can only imagine her glancing over her shoulder, her hands cutting through the water as she silently gives directions. A cruel version of communication that bullies used to sneak up on me when I was younger, but little did they know, their jests would only make me stronger.

There's a trickle of warmth in my system, and suddenly, I understand.

"It's happened," I whisper. I tilt my head down, giving her a smirk. "And when you need a hero, when you need the tides to shift, you'll find yourself untying me."

"Narsana!" Someone else's voice explodes through the room. "Narsana, the Guardians…they're attacking our people."

"What?" Narsana exits my personal space. "Explain yourself."

"The Seraphic Item, it—it's not right. It's changed the Guardians into…into monsters. Nothing works against them. They can't be stopped."

There's a weight you learn when all eyes are on you. A sixth sense picking up on the gazes of each being, their thoughts pressing against your skin as they wait for you to say something more, finally believing what you've told them. My mother always spoke about it, telling me I had a gift at feeling the touch of the intangible.

My smile widens. "Tell me again, Narsana, how God would ever use someone as filthy as me?"

Hours. That's how long I'm left alone, tied up in utter silence. Sometimes the world shakes, telling me a battle has erupted. Just as I'd predicted three years ago. The Seraphic Item had been tainted. It was to be our downfall.

But no one heeded my warnings.

I rub my wrists to soothe the stinging. I'd freed myself a while ago, my body aching from this upright position. The tether around my tail was more difficult to wiggle out of, but I managed with minimal damage. I was never like my mother: easy-going, pleasant, and delicate. I was more like my late father: rough, callous, and sharp-edged. Being unable to see brought me hardships I'd wish upon no one else, creating this rough diamond I've become.

But those in charge find favor in out-casting those that don't fit their agenda.

I lie against the cold ground, stretching my back. I owe these people nothing, even if my heart insists on helping otherwise. They wronged me, but they're still the building blocks to who I became. They are family, even if I'd rather let them stew in their wrongdoings.

So when Narsana falls into my area, breathing heavily and reeking of blood, I give a heavy exhale.

"Took you long enough. Thought you might have died."

"Why did you think I'd come to you for help? You can't touch the Item; you aren't a Guardian."

"I was, but I was blind, so you denied God's will. And then my mother's ability was passed down to me, and you called me crazy and a murderer." I turn my head in her direction, the room quaking. "I said that because you need me."

"Why?" she asks, her voice strained with pain. "Why you?"

"Because I'm a product of my parents." I give a soft smile. "An Oracle *and* a Guardian."

Narsana hisses a laugh. "And why would that be of any help when the Oracle tells of the future and the Guardians have been corrupted?"

I sit up, lacing my webbed fingers together and setting them in my lap. "Because I'm the only one that can touch the Seraphic Item, live, and not be taken by the blight."

I don't need sight to know how to get to the Seraphic Item.

The spheroid pulsates with dark energy. Everything in my being reacts to it, doing its best to not absorb the negativity as I near it, its pull getting stronger. Whispers that don't belong to bodies fill my ears, but I pay no mind to them. Hearing them in a weakened state is what did my mother in.

Narsana gasps as she stops in the entrance. "What happened? Why is it black?"

I've heard the Seraphic Item glows gold normally. If it's black, that means its at its worst state: unstable.

"Inviting demons in your home opens doors you should never walk through," I answer. "The more we play God, the further we drift from Him."

"Quit babbling and answer my question."

"The Seraphic Item is a delicate gift. It can only take so much evil before it's corrupted." I put a hand out, telling her to stay back. "And now we have to remove it."

"Remove it?" Narsana repeats, but I say nothing else.

"Anamara!"

Toru has arrived.

"If you're here for apologies, it's too late," I tell him as he passes Narsana.

My fingers touch the blazing hot surface of the spheroid. Only Oracles and the chosen ones, the Guardians, can lay hands on the Seraphic Item. The Guardians are imbued with the power to protect our people from harm.

Scales stretch from my tail to the rest of my body as I grow and grow, my muscles expanding and growing, my bones shifting within. My arms stretch, hands turning to claws as my face lengthens, and vibrations create sketchy images in my mind. My size grows tenfold, my teeth sharpening as I let out a roar. The soundwaves shake everything, giving me a clearer picture of my surroundings: a huge cave with an opening at the top so the Guardians can get out without wrecking the rest of the area.

"You really are a Guardian," Narsana breathes as I reach down with a claw and pluck the spheroid from its place. Warmth fills my transformed body as instructions run through my mind. I clutch the spheroid tightly.

"Don't look for me," I instruct before making my way to the hole and bursting out.

Blood and fear thicken the water, roars and grunts ceasing as I come to a halt, treading the current as attention turns to me, a roar exploding from my belly. The village is fleeing, what's left of it. Five massive Guardians stand around me, focused on my presence. I let out another roar, receiving another shaky image, putting the descriptions I've always heard to what I see in my mind.

A creature with eight legs—an octopus. Kamins. A monster with the body of a whale but the jaws of a shark, a creature we call a crygrar. That would be Jaksul. Then there's Nebar, her Guardian form a long snout with a powerful tail, spinous processes all across the back. Persan, who has a shark body and seven deadly, serpentine heads. And Nami, a giant worm-like creature with a round mouth made of nothing but teeth, a creature we call a zarkog.

"This is the end of the Guardians," I bellow, hoping someone will listen as we pass through the eye of the chaos storm. "Take care of your hearts, as they are susceptible to corruption."

I lift the spheroid as I sense the Guardians rushing toward me, drawn in by the Seraphic Item.

I turn and swim as far as I can, my transformed body not tiring easily. I have no idea where I'm going; all I can do is use this newfound echolocation to occasionally "see" where I am, if you can call it that. Even then, the water gets too deep for there to be anything soundwaves can bounce off.

I find myself muttering about how if they'd have just left me in peace, then these unnecessary deaths would have been avoided. I'd protect the Seraphic Item and they'd live on, becoming better and stronger, and drawing nearer to God instead of relying on Guardians and Oracles to protect them from enemies and an Oracle to use as an excuse to sin.

Eventually, the Guardians tire, too exhausted to fight over the spheroid. I lead them into a cave system, their bodies shifting into their normal, mermadic selves. Usually, they have full control in Guardian form, but with the blight in the Item, they lost themselves. The corruption is what my mother feared. When she saw a speck of darkness in the Item, she took it for herself so it wouldn't spread, taking on the sins of our people so they wouldn't suffer. But just that little bit of darkness drove her insane.

Drove her to nearly killing her child.

But I'm not like my mother. For too long, our village has pushed their sins onto one person, letting them take the blame. It's time for them to reap what they've sown. It's time for them to learn and grow.

The Guardians' eyes struggle to stay open as they lift off the ground. Their questions reach my ears as I hold the spheroid with my claw, standing before them with my tail coiled around me.

"A dragon," Nebar whispers, her words slurred with exhaustion.

I explain to them what had transpired, horrified expressions filtering through their fatigue.

"If you wish to return home, you may, but I request your assistance in guarding the Item with your lives. This is an unbreakable tool of both destruction and life, and I fear those who hear about it will stop at nothing to have it, especially those we left behind." I stand taller. "This is my calling, why I was born. Would you stand with me to protect the integrity of both our people and this world?"

Years pass. Indeed, there are many creatures that come for the spheroid. Little by little, the blight in the Item fades, according to my companions. They learn to control their Guardian bodies once again as they guard their heart and keep their mind sharp. It gets easier the more the Seraphic Item looks like it should.

"How much is left?" I ask Kamins one day as he climbs the pillar I keep the spheroid on.

"It looks like it's nearly gone." He hesitates as I climb out of my little hole and swim closer to him. "Don't you miss home?"

"I have no home on this Earth," I reply. "Are you wishing to leave?"

"No, I believe my duty is here, I just… Why would you give up a life for our village, when all they did is force you out?"

I let his question sink in before I sigh. "Because it's the right thing to do."

"Intruders!"

My head snaps around to Jaksul's voice echoing throughout the cave system. I hear Kamins push off to assist the others, leaving me alone with the Seraphic Item. I am the last line of defense before the intruders can take the spheroid. If I fall, I will bring this whole place down with me. If they survive, it's God's will.

The sounds of battle never reach me, and panic floods my system. Have the other Guardians been slain without a fight?

I swim to tread before the Item, honing in on the moving water. Just one creature, swimming like a merperson. All I can think is, *so this is how I die.*

The merperson reaches my area.

"Leave, or face death."

"I'd rather have death than never seeing you again."

I freeze, my scales rustling as a shiver works its way through my bones. That voice…

"Why have you come? Are you here to betray me once more, Toru?"

"I searched for you for five years, teamed up with surface dwellers… Do you really think that would be the reason?"

"If you're here to kill me, make it swift like you did the others. I—"

"I didn't kill them." He pauses, swimming closer. "I told them why I'm here."

"And why is that, if not for the Item?"

"To apologize and make amends. I didn't know what else to do. My family… Removing the Seraphic Item caused a plague, and the surrounding villages raided, draining our resources. The Guardians couldn't protect us properly and we lost many, including my family. And when you finally returned with it, when the Guardians touched it, they nearly took out the rest."

"So you're here to guilt trip me?"

"No."

I jump as his hand touches my snout, the gesture comforting in a strange way.

"I'm sorry. You were my best friend and I was your only, and I betrayed you. I should have never given you up."

I snort. "It only took you seven years to realize it. But I appreciate the apology. Now go, before you overstay your welcome."

"I'll come to visit."

"Don't."

"Someone has to keep you company."

"I have the Guardians," I reply, whipping my tail impatiently.

"But you don't love any of them like you love me."

I'm struck into silence, my tail the only thing moving as my nerves alight. He's always been my favorite merperson; I guess he picked up on that as well.

He touches my face once more, warmth spreading through my body as I receive the fact I can trust him, that he learned his lesson and is genuinely reaching out.

"I won't let you die alone."

With that, he's gone, and I can't utter a single word.

"What happens when my uncles and aunties die?"

I lean forward, placing a finger over my mouth as I suppress my smirk. "Don't let them hear you, dear. Death can be frightening to some people."

"Happy eighth birthday, Angel." Toru kisses our daughter on the forehead; I can tell by the way she groans quietly and wipes it away.

"The new Guardians will find you. They normally are offspring of the originals."

"So much for the end of the Guardians and Oracles," Toru comments as he sits beside us, handing something to Angel. Her birthday gift, no doubt. He said he made something for her, a trinket to match my own remade homing device. She gushes over it as I comment on Toru's aside.

"It was the end for our village," I correct. "But the Item is indestructible. Even if we buried or hid it, greedy creatures would just find it once more. If we feed it to a monster, it will eventually become excrement, waiting for the next."

Angel rushes down to play with the children the other Guardians created with one another or spouses they convinced to come with them to live with us. We live in our own little tight-knit community, all nineteen of us, and we protect the Seraphic Item from falling into harm's hands.

"Intruder!" Persan calls, and I hear everyone getting into position: the Guardians rising to touch the Item and the children and non-Guardian spouses getting into their hideaways.

As I kiss Toru on the cheek, I give him a smile. Before I can join the rest, he grabs my arm to pull me back.

"Be careful."

I kiss him on the mouth and give a smile. Never did I think my life would turn out like this—and I wouldn't want it any other way.

"Always am."

I join the Guardians, our hands touching the spheroid. Our bodies shift and grow as we prepare to put our lives on the line for those we love and the world we live in. An octopus, a crygrar, a crocodile, a hydra, a zarkog, and a sea dragon: the Guardians of the Seraphic Item.

WICKED WASTELANDERS

Nathaniel Luscombe

Pain swelled along the tips of my ears. It burned, making it hard for me to concentrate. I couldn't stop thinking about the pain. The ear-cuffs tucked the pointed end in, hiding it behind the gilded bands that ran down both sides of my face. It was the easiest way to disguise the fact that I was an elf. While I still held a grace that humans would never truly master, and the structure of my face was more angular, I could play it all off as something I attained through practice and surgery.

My ears, though, were one hundred percent an elf thing. There was no denying it.

I lingered on the edge of the party. While it had been advertised as a modest gathering, the crowd of a thousand rich people totally ruined the vibe.

Plus, we were on a glass floor floating on the surface of the ocean. If the rumor was true that the budget was close to a million dollars, it could not be called a modest gathering. It meant there were good pickings. While I wasn't a picker myself, I'd brought several of them along.

This was the last stretch in funding our escape from this watery hell. Nothing good came from water planets.

"You look distracted," Kerial said. She walked up and clasped my hand, drawing her body in close. "Have you heard anything?"

I shook my head. My ear-cuffs also doubled as a radio. Somewhere, in a small sub beneath the surface, Curi was planning the climax of the party. It wasn't something the hosts had planned, but I was looking forward to throwing it into their itinerary.

"We've got enough to make the trip worth it. The cloak room alone is more than I thought we would get from the whole night." She smiled, her sharp teeth edging onto her lips. While she held the grace and beauty that all elves did, there was a sharp side to her that scared me. She would bite me as quickly as she would heal me.

"Are you saying you thought my plan would fail?" I slouched and let out a small pout, pretending to be hurt.

She elbowed me and laughed. "I always sit on the negative side. You have exceeded my expectations." She planted a light kiss on my lips and strode off into the crowd.

If I wasn't distracted before, I was now. I followed her as she crossed the room. She was the sun in this dark universe, and somehow I couldn't tear my eyes away from her. I couldn't deny the feelings that I had for her. She seemed to know too, playing with my emotions like she was testing me.

The crowd grew thick, pressing against the wall. I leaned against the cool glass and waited for it to disperse. Small pockets of air traveled above our heads as the more important guests made their way through the people. There were the rich ones, and then there were the important ones.

Money bought a place at the gathering, but importance bought respect.

One of the air pockets broke near me, the people moving out of the way for an imposing figure. I recognized her as Vyrleen Laeger, the one hosting this gathering. She approached a few people, shaking hands and exchanging hugs, before her eyes locked with mine. I saw it there, the momentary confusion followed by a steeled look. Vyrleen was not used to mistakes at her gatherings. If she didn't recognize someone, it was usually because of her poor memory and not the fact that they were here to crash her event.

She started walking toward me. I knew she meant to talk to me, so I turned and hurried off into the crowd. My team was better at what they did, faking their stories and meeting expectations of strangers. I was likely to screw up the whole mission. Even though it was my plan, I wasn't sure I was the best to carry it out.

"Verne, are you there?" Curie's soft voice broke through the cuff. I smiled, hoping that Vyrleen wasn't wanting to talk to me. A quick glance behind me showed that she'd moved on to someone else, her little bubble moving farther from me.

"I'm here. How's it going?"

"I found one. I just need to get it into position. How much longer do you need?" His voice grew fuzzy and he grunted.

"Is everything okay?"

There was silence. Then, "Yeah, I just didn't expect it to give me this much trouble."

"I'll find someone and see how much more time they need."

He didn't respond. The connection between me and his sub was not good, and we didn't have time to make it better. The sub wasn't even ours. It came from a cheap rental, the last option we'd had.

I walked along the edge, keeping one hand close to the wall. I didn't like to be fully surrounded by people. I felt like an illusion. Being human was easy, but only when I was in full control of what people saw. When surrounded, it was harder to maintain a perfect cover.

If tonight went well, I wouldn't have to pretend for a long time. While most elves worked beneath the humans as glorified slaves, there were still a few free factions. We called ourselves the Wastelanders. The humans tolerated our kind because of our abilities. But we couldn't use such abilities here without risking human technology tracking our gifts. All we needed to do was steal enough jewelry to sell so that we could get on a ship and take off into the universe.

No destination. No ruler. Just our people. A safe haven that others could escape to eventually.

For now, we focused on the first step: attaining the ship. We had run several scams, but this was the most elaborate. The rich didn't mess around when it came to their money, but they also didn't feel threatened when surrounded by their own.

I caught sight of Gadriel. He was the third elf here. Three was the limit, and even that felt risky. In a crowd of a thousand, we had to fool everyone into thinking we were just like them. Fortunately, he was good at it. With a drink in one hand and a human girl in the other, he fit in with the crowd. Only I noticed the way his hand slipped her necklace off, a flash of gold that vanished down his sleeve. He spun her out, his eyes warm as they explored her face, and pulled her back in for another embrace.

I walked up and tapped him on the shoulder. He turned and the girl looked at me.

"Do you want to dance with him?" she asked, smiling.

"Uh, yes. Would you dance with me?"

Gadriel chuckled. "It would be my pleasure." He took my arm and we left the girl behind. "That was real smooth, my boy."

I laughed. We took our place as the music made its way through the crowd. I recognized the tone. It was the type of music that came from a starsinger. There was another elf on board.

"I didn't realize there was a starsinger here," I murmured.

"Don't look at him too much, but I was going to see if we could get him out of here." Gadriel spun out, his eyes twinkling with amusement. We were both used to playing the lead when it came to dancing.

"I have never seen a starsinger at work." I couldn't help but admire the musician. He sat nearby on a pedestal, his feet hanging over the edge. As his voice filled the air, so did the twinkling of magic. The light was caught on the end of the music. It danced in its own way, spiraling between the feet of the people. The dark floor reflected the light in an eerie way. The people were enthralled. It was sickening, the way they loved magic but hated the magician.

"Well, I know you didn't dance with me to watch the starsinger."

"Curie wants to know when we'll be done."

"Last time I talked to Kerial, she was almost at her limit. I can't hide a lot more either, so he could come at any time."

"Perfect." I spun away from him and melded back into the crowd. I tapped the cuff and Curie's breathing filled my ear. "You can come now. We're done."

"I'm on my way."

So now I had to wait. That was the worst part, knowing what was going to happen, but not knowing when. My heart picked up and I shook a little. It would be best if we were all within sight of each other. I continued making rounds along the edge, keeping an eye out for the others. I finally saw Kerial's slender form standing above the rest, her head nodding as she listened to someone speak.

Gadriel sidled up next to me. "Okay, I'm done."

"Curie's on his way. I just need to grab Kerial and then we wait." I moved my fingers anxiously. My ear was starting to burn, an itch working its way through the tip. I shuddered, trying not to react. The itchiness wasn't going away.

Kerial turned around and spotted us. Her eyes lit up and she waved. At that moment, the world dropped beneath my feet. I fell, the startled screams of other guests filling the closed space. I got onto my hands and knees and looked at the water beneath the glass. Instead of the deep blue, it was now a hazy red.

Curie had done his work. The beast was here.

I was about to stand when it came into view, open-mouthed and angry. Its face rammed into the glass and it turned, dashing toward the center of the room. I scrambled back, my heart pounding. The infamous white sharks that infested these water planets were known to grow large, but this one was bigger than I imagined. It was almost the size of a whale.

The other guests let out shrieks as they caught sight of the monster beneath their feet. The water was full of a mixture of blood and small parts of fish. The creature would be here for a while. The floor tilted again as it rammed into the glass.

Gadriel pulled me off the floor. "Come on, let's see if we can get the starsinger."

I followed him through the crowd, hoping that Kerial would see us and come after us. The guests were too frantic to notice the two men running for the pedestal. The starsinger sat on top, clutching the edges, his knuckles white.

"Do you need help down?" Gadriel shouted.

"I can't come down. I'm chained."

I saw it then, the glittering piece of metal holding him to the pedestal. When he sang, it looked like part of his magic.

Kerial emerged from the crowd. "What's taking you two so long? This isn't where we were supposed to meet."

The starsinger seemed to clue in. His eyes grew bright with excitement and magic filled the air around us. He edged toward us, his feet kicking at the chain. "This is your fault. Are you here to save me?"

I closed my eyes, horror filling the pit in my stomach. I couldn't stand seeing my own people in bondage and not being able to help. But we couldn't take him with us. The chain could only be opened by his mistress, and we had no way of getting that to happen.

"We will come back," I said. "Not today, but someday. We will get you away from your mistress and back with your people."

He was crying. I wouldn't believe me if I was him, but I had no other choice. We only had one chance to get out of here.

The floor bucked more than it had before. I slipped, catching a glimpse of several fins. There were more sharks now, large and hungry. They filled the water beneath the floor with their thirst for blood.

"There are ships coming to take us back to Skyline." The monotonous voice filled the room. Skyline was the floating city that made its way around the small planet. If they were getting involved, that meant this was serious. For a moment, I fell victim to fear. We may have not just disrupted the party. If they were evacuating, it meant the situation was more serious than I realized.

"The room is tilting." Gadriel cursed.

"The sharks damaged something and now it can't float, I guess." Unlike Gadriel, Kerial seemed pleased. I didn't blame her. It felt good to do damage to something that the humans took pride in.

"Come on. Curie is meeting us at the rendezvous point." We left the starsinger on his pedestal and hurried toward the entrance. As ridiculous as it sounded, there was an outside to this crazy glass craft. Tall walls separated the water from this elite world, but there was access that would lead us to Curie's ship.

I risked one glance back before exiting and saw Vyrleen freeing the starsinger. Guards surrounded him, keeping him from joining us. I now knew who owned him. I vowed to track him down and keep my promise of freedom.

Vicious wind roared when we stepped outside. Some of the guests saw what we were doing and tried to follow. I hurried to the edge of the platform and looked at the water. Kerial and Gadriel held onto me to stop me from slipping as the sharks continued in their feeding frenzy.

"Curie, we're waiting." I spoke into the cuff, but the wind snatched my words. The water lapped against the glass, bloody water running past my hands. I felt it now, the way the glass surrendered to the water, sinking beneath the waves that called its name. I'd never meant to sink this place. I just wanted freedom and a way to grant it to my people.

The first transports from Skyline emerged from the clouds. Their soft searchlights illuminated the dark water, reflecting off the sides of the glass. The humans surged towards them, wanting to be the first off the ship.

A fin sliced through the water. Gadriel pulled me back, but the large creature pushed against the edge and I slipped on the wet glass. A startled shriek clawed out of my throat before I fell into the water.

I tasted the blood immediately. It filled my mouth as I frantically reached for the surface. While the sharks wouldn't purposely eat me, I don't think they would mind if I was snagged among the other pieces of food. I got above the surface and grabbed for the edge of the platform. My fingers couldn't find purchase on the glass. Gadriel grabbed my hand, but I could see that he was starting to slip too.

The water next to me bubbled and Curie's sub rose to the surface. Kerial leaped from the glass to the sub and opened the hatch. She clambered around the side and grabbed my arm. The water around me moved, a shark swimming right past me. I shuddered and swam for the sub, letting her pull me out of the water. Gadriel jumped and held onto one of the handles.

I followed them into the sub. It was small, only meant to carry five people. I settled into one of the chairs. Curie looked over from the controls. "Swimming with the sharks?" He laughed.

"I don't want to talk about it." I shivered. I was wet, and the distinct smell of blood clung to my clothes. I still tasted it on my tongue.

"Then let's get out of here," he said, closing the hatch. The sub hissed before sinking into the great ocean.

It was all over the news. Vyrleen Laeger was injured, and one of her guests had died after an accident sank their party. She was painted across the news as a saint.

She was the last to leave the party, herding everyone out before her, and even helped pay for the trauma caused by her infamous night.

The elves, on the other hand, were painted as devils. Everywhere I turned, there was an article calling for stricter measures and an organized hunt for any Wastelanders. They didn't seem to realize that our actions were a result of their attempt to control us.

I was still shaken by the events of the night. My plan had worked, in theory, but not the way I'd wanted it to. Now, I was drawing negative attention toward my people. It was a rather unfortunate turn of events, but one that hardly seemed avoidable.

"Is there anything I can get you, sir?" A waiter walked over, a tray of drinks in his hand.

"No, I'm good." I held up a hand and smiled. He backed away and bowed.

The service here was nice. With the money we had, we were able to afford a couple nights on the Starliner, a space station meant to house travelers. It was our last human stop before we took to the stars.

I scratched at my ear-cuff. Kerial was bartering with the man in charge of scraps, trying to find us a ship that was space-worthy. Surprisingly, a lot of people threw away good ships for no reason. The Starliner had a whole level of abandoned ships that were for sale.

Curie stepped up beside me. He sipped his drink and sighed. "What's on your mind?" He glanced at me.

"I'm worried about a lot of things. The future, mostly."

"Don't. Kerial will get us a ship and we'll leave all of this behind." He seemed so sure of it, but I knew that our plan was not foolproof. It was hardly a plan. If anyone wanted to find us, I was sure they could.

"And if it doesn't work out?"

"The worst they can do is bring us back to that godforsaken water planet. I think we're going to be fine." He clapped my back and grinned. "Loosen up a bit. Our journey has only begun."

I took his glass and drank a big gulp. It raced like fire down my throat, filling me with life. I would not be held back by past mistakes. Once we had a ship, the entire universe would be at our fingertips.

We just had to choose the first destination.

LAND BEYOND THE SEA

A gender-swapped Tír na nÓg meets Cinderella

Cheyenne van Langevelde

THE spring sun shone blindingly on the rippling waves as they rolled onto the shore, leaving broken bits of shells in their wake. The wind sang in response across the dunes and through the forest beyond, blowing kisses at the sea whose waters caressed the land. A love most sacred and binding, unlike Niamh's broken family.

Tears coursed down her face, their cool wetness a balm to her heated face. Sadly, they had no healing power to touch the bruises mottling her back. Regardless of her efforts, she could never live up to the expectations of her brothers and father—who were not her own by blood. Were it not for her mother needing a strong helper, she would have held true to the memory of her first love. But she had needed Cillian, needed his aid in keeping the land alive to support herself and their new family.

Niamh stumbled along the beach, her footsteps sinking into the soft, warm sand.

Yet need did not necessarily mean love, and while Cillian might have loved her mother and his sons by another marriage, his heart had not had room for Niamh. And now that her mother was gone, he had not gentled his gaze towards her, nor had her new brothers gained any compassion. No, what affection they had translated itself in blows and mockery, giving her the heaviest chores as if to see how far they could push her before she would break.

She collapsed onto the sand and buried her face in her arms. The sun beat down from cloudless skies and the wind toyed with her black hair, whispering wordless comfort in her ears. The sea crept up to her feet and dared to touch her, giving the only tenderness she could have from anyone.

A tragic thing, that the only love she could receive was that from the untameableness of nature, and not from the steadfastness of humanity.

Perhaps her father and brothers were indeed heartless, but her sensitive nature shied from thinking so ill of them—even if they deserved it. Her mother had raised her to be kind, to think the best of everyone, to show compassion and tenderness regardless of station. But when they beat her and teased her as she struggled to complete her tasks, she nearly broke from the strain.

Niamh raised her head and sat up, sand slipping down the folds of her dress. It would not do to cry, for it did little to improve her situation aside from momentary relief. She rose to her feet and gazed at the blue horizon in the distance where the deep grey of the sea met the pale sapphire of sky, a shuddering sigh escaping her lips.

She longed to escape, to be free of the beatings and scorn, to not constantly worry whether she did something good enough to escape her father and brothers' loathing. But she could not swim, not that far. And she did not have a boat by which to sail away.

Perhaps freedom was only a dream after all, an idea, a concept—nothing more.

The soft thud of hoofbeats against sand broke the song of the waves against the shore.

Niamh turned in surprise, for they never received visitors, and certainly not from the direction of the sea. She squinted against the bright sun, her hand shielding her eyes from its light as the rider drew near.

The man reined in his horse once they drew alongside her and dismounted. Without a word spoken, he dropped to his knee and took her hand, kissing it gently.

Niamh stared at him in horror. No one had ever done so to her, a mere peasant. What new devilry was this?

"*Le do thoil*, Niamh, do not be afraid." His voice was soft yet powerful, like the waves lapping onto the shore that had the capacity to roar during a storm.

"How do you know my name?" she gasped, as afraid of him as ever. His words, though spoken pleadingly, had done nothing to console her. Perhaps her father had given her away in marriage for a price like he had threatened to do the last several months. Her heart stuck in her throat for terror.

"Niamh, my name is Oisín. I come from the land over the sea, the land of Tír na nÓg." He paused to thrust a strand of crimson-gold hair out of his eyes that the wind tossed there, tucking it behind one of his delicately pointed ears.

Niamh stared at him, wonder washing away her fear. Tír na nÓg was a land of faerie lore, a place where Time had no say, a land of eternal youth and love and beauty. Her mother had sung about it to her as a child, but she had never believed it was real. Not until now.

"I have watched you for years, watching you grow up from the shy child that shadowed your mother, who believed in the old stories, into a beautiful young woman who"—he cast a nervous glance into the trees hiding the croft from view—"is bound to serve by those who do not love her."

Her mouth tightened. As much as she longed to believe those words, to accept the compliment from this handsome stranger, whose eyes sparkled like the sea, something held her back. She knew her own mind; aye, she would not fall for flattery.

"Forgive me, Oisín, but how am I supposed to trust you?" Her voice was cold in her own ears, as cold as the ocean's depths.

His eyes darkened, a blue-grey of unsettled waves. "I have no token of trust, only my word of honour. I mean you no harm. I…" His voice faltered and he looked at the sand at their feet, the sun shadowing his freckled high cheekbones and strong jawline. "I have seen how your father and brothers treat you and I wish to rescue you from them—if you will have me."

"And where would you take me?" The skepticism remained, but something pulled in her chest to trust him.

All the same, what was said about the promises of the fae?

"To Tír na nÓg, of course!" A nervous chuckle escaped his lips and he glanced up to meet her eyes shyly. "Where else would I take you?" His horse nickered as if in agreement.

Niamh looked away towards the house she knew lay within the darkening shadows of the woods. She could refuse this Oisín and his promises of freedom and eternal youth. And for what? Had she not been lamenting her fate in life just moments before? Did she want to return to that, to endless shaming and ridicule and hatred?

Was it worth the risk?

"You promised your honour," she finally said. "On what do you swear it? Honour is a fine thing, but it means nothing if there is nothing to bind it with."

Oisín knelt on the sand, his horse's reins falling slack. He gazed earnestly into her face and clasped his hands over his heart. "I swear it on my honour as a Fae and on the secret kept hidden from mortals. But I do not swear it solely on my honour, but on my love for you as I have watched you these many years and kept this shore safe from those who would wish you and your mother harm." His face fell. "But harm came from inland, where we no longer hold sway… I wish to remedy those wrongs as best as I may. My people have offered a place for you among them; you will no longer be an outcast."

A place to belong. It seemed unreal. Could it be true?

"Niamh!" Cillian shouted her name from the woods. She had been absent far too long.

Her heart hammered in her throat as Oisín rose to his feet and watched her, waiting still for an answer. She wanted to think about this and avoid making a wrong decision out of haste.

But time was not her ally.

"I will go with you," she finally said, swallowing the fear that twisted within her. "Yet we must hurry. They will reach the shore within moments."

Without a word spoken, Oisín offered her his arm and lifted her into the saddle. He climbed up deftly in front of her and dug his heels into the flank of his horse, who whinnied in delight and plunged into the waves.

Sea spray flew into her face, the salty drops kissing her in welcome. Niamh buried her face in Oisín's back as she clung to him, fleeing the only place she had ever known.

Cillian cried out in alarm as he broke onto the beach and saw them riding away into the ocean, but he could not pursue them. Neither he nor his sons could swim.

The surf came up to their legs as the horse pushed on, the wind singing in their ears. And then the sea itself parted for them and the cloudless skies broke into the golden light of another world long-forgotten and hidden from mortal eyes.

Niamh shut her eyes against the brightness lest it blind her, a comforting warmth kissing her skin like the sun itself enlivened her veins. The air was sweet with the heavy scent of blossoming flowers, but it lacked the bittersweetness of the sea—which she was accustomed to breathing her whole life; she felt its absence sharply.

The horse stopped moving beneath her and she opened her eyes to see a much younger, brighter sun shining down on a world emblazoned in verdant splendour. Flowers thrived everywhere the eye could see, their myriad colours revealing every hue Niamh could imagine. Water cascaded down a cliffside into a pool below where children swam and splashed each other. Couples of all years of youth walked beneath the flowering trees or sat on mossy rocks, some dangling their feet into the rippling stream. The place radiated joy and peace, something Niamh had not had much of.

Oisín dismounted and helped her down, a smile on his face. "Welcome to Tír na nÓg, *grá geal mo chroí.*"

As if he had summoned them, a train of girls dressed in pastel colours and wearing wreathed flowers in their hair came forward, leading her away into her new life in the land of eternal youth, the land beyond the sea.

Time did not pass, for time did not exist in Tír na nÓg. Time was irrelevant in a place where youth was eternal. Time was marked solely by marriage and birth of children who grew up to be beautiful lasses and lads who in turn married and had young ones of their own.

But Niamh was happy. No one burdened her with tasks that spent her strength. No one belittled her, nor reminded her how worthless nor how much of a burden she was. She was loved, loved and adored by Oisín and their three fair children.

She only missed one thing from her old life, and that was the sea. In the land of immortality, a land where time itself held no sway, the ocean did not exist. The ocean, which wore away at the land, slowly reclaiming it for its own, belonged to a world where time wore itself away, one grain of sand through the hourglass at a time. Change, in its waves and storms of life, had no power in Tír na nÓg.

She missed the tang of salt burning her lips, the hollow cry of the waves crashing onto the beach, the waters sparkling beneath the sun. Sometimes, the wind would gust across the flower meadows in Tír na nÓg, the rippling grass resembling the surf rushing onto the land, and the homing hunger stung her heart.

And such longing only grew as days of pure bliss passed.

Humans were meant to experience the billows of life, love and heartache, the changing weathers and times, for they are meant to endure despite the hardships.

The fae merely existed. Surrounded in a safe world where only the perfect present happened, depth was missing from their happiness. True happiness is all the more meaningful for the times of grief before it. The fae did not grieve; their happiness was shallow inebriation in comparison with human joy, sweetened by loss.

The hardest part was that no one—not even Oisín—understood.

"*Mo grá*, what are these tears upon your face?" Oisín's fingers gently brushed Niamh's face, warm against the cold tears slipping down her face against her will.

She shrugged her shoulders and wiped the tears away, inhaling sharply. She was glad no one else could see her; no one ever cried in Tír na nÓg because there was no reason for them to. Life was perfect here. "I confess I do not know."

He looked into her eyes with pity. "Surely there must be a reason. Has anyone been unkind to you? Are the children alright? Is it something you need?"

Niamh shook her head. "Nay, 'tis from no wrong here. Your people have shown me nothing but utter kindness. And the children are fine. I…" Her voice faltered.

"You can tell me, my love." He enveloped her in a sweet embrace, holding her close but not crushing her.

"I miss the sea." It was out at last, the secret she had kept hidden for so long.

"The sea?" He stiffened in confusion.

"Aye. I had spent my entire life by it. And there is no such thing here; I have missed it ever since I first came here, a longing that has only grown through time until 'tis nearly unbearable."

Oisín did not answer for a time.

Niamh closed her eyes tightly, wondering with sickening fear whether her ungratefulness had offended him. He had never found cause to be displeased with her before, but perhaps expressing a fault with the perfect world he had brought her to was a transgression he could not forgive.

"There is a chance, a slim one at best, that you can return for a time."

Hope rose in her heart and could not be repressed. "How?"

"My horse will take you back, if the elders allow it. But only for a moment of time and you must never touch the ground."

Niamh pulled back and squinted at him in the dimness of their home. "How so?"

Oisín pursed his lips. "*Mo grá*, the world you left has not stood still. We do not notice the passing of time in Tír na nÓg, but out there, the world continues to wear away. It will not be the same place you remember." His crimson brows drew together in worry—an emotion rarely seen in this place. "I fear that if you go, you will not return."

"And why would I not? All I love is here. I only miss the sea and wonder what became of the world I left behind."

He sighed heavily. "I will speak to the elders and let you know what they say. But do not trust to hope. No one has ever been allowed to return before." He left her standing in the doorway.

She shivered, feeling cold despite the warm sunshine spilling from the cloudless sky.

Was her longing truly worth such a sacrifice and a risk?

The morning dawned cool and bright, the first fingers of light brushing away the night.

Oisín readied his horse in silence, most of the fae still sleeping. The sun had not yet risen, but he and Niamh were already awake, she with cloaked donned for the journey.

"There, she should bear you safely enough." He patted the mare's neck and turned to his wife. "Promise me you will return."

Worry was not something Niamh was accustomed to, not anymore, and especially from her beloved husband. "Why would I not return? 'Tis only the sea I miss. Everything else is here."

"I only do not wish for anything to happen to you." He kissed her forehead gently. "That is all."

"'Tis only Éire, *mo grá*," she murmured, throwing her arms around him in farewell. "There is no reason anything would happen. Nothing happens there. I will come back, I promise." She kissed him and then mounted the horse.

"*Slán go fóill!*" Oisín called out as she rode out of the village and the land of Tír na nÓg.

The doorway opened from meadow to sea, from sun to storm, from Tír na nÓg to Éire, from eternity into time.

The horse stepped through and the coming wave hid the portal from view. Niamh inhaled sharply the gust of salty breeze and tears sprang to her eyes. How she had missed it!

She spurred the horse onward and away from the strong tide of the waves. The sea roared in greeting and thunder echoed its welcoming cry. The trees sang out in the breeze and the surf sprayed across her face.

The mare neighed as her hooves touched the dry sand of the high beach and no longer struggled against the undertow. Niamh looked out across the horizon, no less familiar from being so long away.

Lightning flashed in the distance, white against the darkness of storm clouds. Thunder rumbled in reply and the sea rushed anon upon the beach, frothy waves rising on the shell-laced sand.

Niamh resisted the sudden urge to dismount and touch the sand with her feet, to feel the ground where she had walked and wept before. But she had promised Oisín she would not do so. All the same, she longed to.

She glanced behind her as the rising wind caught at her hair, shrieking its way into the wood behind her. It was denser and darker than she remembered, the ground thick with underbrush that she had no memory of existing before. She wondered whether the croft still stood, whether Cillian and Brochan and Donal and Séan still lived in that place, or whether they had removed inland to the towns she had never seen.

She dug her heels into the mare's flanks, trying to spur her into the woods, but the mare neighed fiercely, nostrils flaring as she tossed her mane in defiance.

Niamh bit her lip. Not like they would have cared anyway. Curiosity helped no one.

She was about to return to the waves and the coming storm when a shout echoed through the woods. Unfamiliar voices called out in reply, their language strange and foreign to her ears. That was not the Gaeilge she was used to.

"Come on, Aileen," she whispered in the mare's ears, not wanting to be discovered. "Let's go home."

The horse trotted towards the waves, which now tossed to and fro across the surface, white caps flickering across the dark blue. The wind was nearly constant now, roaring in her ears, louder than the growing thunder.

Figures broke through the trees, armed with strange weapons that glistened in the flash of lightning that crackled above their heads. They spoke to one another hurriedly and in a moment, had surrounded Niamh and her mare. They seized the reins out of her hands and threw questions at her which she did not understand.

"Let me go! I have done you no harm!" she cried to no avail.

They laughed at her and one of them yanked her off of the horse's back, the mare shrieking in terror. Niamh screamed as she touched the sand, cool beneath her bare feet.

And then she was gone, dissipated to dust within their hands.

The horse broke free and dashed for the waves, disappearing into a place of light and beauty, leaving behind the storm and the strangers who had brought about Niamh's death.

Oisín was the first to grab his mare's halter, his worst fears now realized.

"*Athair*, where is Mother?" his daughter asked, her face still flushed from sleep. She stood in the doorway, the sun shining on her golden ringlets.

"She's gone, my sweet," he said bitterly, fighting back tears. "She went back to her home and must have touched the earth that was some hundred years older."

His daughter laid her hand on his arm. "You mean…"

"She is not coming back. The earth reclaimed her for its own." He bit back the curse that formed on his lips and led his horse away to the meadow.

And once he was out of sight of his children and the other fae, he wept. Wept for the woman he had loved, for the brief life they had lived, wept for himself and his children, the only fae who would taste death. He grieved for Niamh, his bright love of his heart, who would never again return to the land beyond the sea.

Translation:
~ Le do thoil - please
~ Grá geal mo chroí - love of my life
~ Mo grá - my life
~ Slán go fóill - farewell for now
~ Athair - father

STUCK IN SPACE

Anna Ford

Nadia would have rather jumped in the electric jellyfish tank than spend any time with Julian.

She stared at the rusted lock of the aquarium doors, counting down each second as it ticked by. Six more minutes of waiting, and she could go back to her bunk and forget all about lab arguments and cleaning supplies and ex-boyfriends.

The filtered air circulated through the hallway with the sanitized smell of bleach and disinfectant spray. The double doors at the end of the long, monochrome hallway slid open as Nadia sucked in a breath. Air caught in her throat, clogging her airway. She doubled over, her coughs echoing off the metal walls.

"Are you okay?"

Nadia straightened up and scowled, brushing her bangs out of her eyes and refusing to look toward the person who had spoken. Cutting her bangs was one of those rash hair decisions no one should be allowed to make, but so far she hadn't regretted it.

The person came closer. "This is going to be a long night if you won't even look at me."

Nadia glanced over just to spite him. Her heart caught in her windpipe.

Julian looked *good*, because of course he would. His dark hair fell in messy waves over his forehead, and it seemed as though he'd gotten taller over the last few months. She assumed his shirt was new, because it wasn't one she recognized.

She faltered for a moment, and she wondered if their ship had hit an asteroid belt.

Julian held up the new mop and a bucket of bleach in his hands, eying the entrance to the aquarium. "Can you open the door?"

Nadia wiped her palms against her jeans and pulled out the keycard to the doors. She noticed that the maintenance crew needed to replace the lock, as it beeped weakly when she swiped the keycard. Nadia pushed on the heavy metal, holding the door open as Julian brushed past.

Canned lights lit up the space in succession, revealing large glass tanks stretching a football field's length from the entrance. The sight of it stole her breath.

Sealife from all planets inhabited the space, swimming and floating in glass enclosures made to their exact specifications. An ethereal glow emanated from each tank, highlighting the wondrous animals inside. Nadia had affectionately nicknamed many of the creatures while studying their many features.

George, the bearded squashfish, with his glittering gills and powerful ability to stomp down any prey.

Oriole, the crescent moon creeper who used long tentacles to roam his exhibit.

Henrietta, the stardust sea turtle, with her eggs buried in the sand. Her exhibit was one of the largest, as the baby stardusts needed room to explore once they hatched.

Blue, the lone narwhal, boasting a glittering unicorn's horn. Nadia adored Blue, with his soulful eyes.

Dottie, the spotted fairy-bear with delicate wings and a magnificent brown and white coat. Despite being a mammal, she lived in the aquarium because she spent most of her waking hours underwater, using her wings to propel her large frame.

Having easy access to these amazing creatures was her favorite part of living on a spaceship.

She hoped being forced to share the space with Julian wouldn't ruin her happy place.

Julian seemed to agree. "Why would Peony send us *here*?"

Nadia and Julian had met in the aquarium, had their first date and their first kiss in the aquarium. They'd also had their first fight in the aquarium.

Their most recent fight had not been in the aquarium.

"You've got to appreciate her style of cruel and unusual punishment," replied Nadia. Peony, their marine life professor, lived and breathed sea animals. She also loved confrontation-style discipline.

Julian regarded her with deep brown eyes full of an emotion she couldn't place, eyes that took her back to a night three years prior in this very spot.

It had never been Nadia's intention to fall in love on a spaceship.

When Nadia accepted her invite to spend her post-high school years aboard the star cruiser, she dreamed of studying aquatic life alongside others who were equally fascinated by the many creatures outside their atmosphere. It was an honor to be one of the few students chosen from the moon colony, and she was not about to waste this opportunity.

Enter, Julian. Funny and charming and wicked smart.

And, as she later learned, a liar.

But she didn't know that when she met him. Didn't know when they had their first date at the coffee station near the aquarium, didn't know when he held her hand and pointed out his favorite animals. Didn't know when she saw how his passion for marine life conservation matched with hers for aquatic research.

Didn't know when they watched the stars float by deep into the night.

Didn't know when he'd gazed into her eyes that he was making promises he wouldn't keep.

If she could go back to that night three years ago and do it all over again, she wouldn't.

Mopping the floors and scrubbing the glass of the individual aquariums took longer that Nadia thought it would. The only bonus was getting to spend more time with the creatures inside each exhibit.

It would have been a lonely couple of hours if not for the animals. Nadia and Julian said as little as they could to each other. With each passing second, tension boiled beneath Nadia's skin, mixed with the salty feeling of betrayal.

Just as Nadia hung up the mop, she heard a metallic clinking behind her. She turned with a reprimand on the tip of her tongue, annoyance seeping under her skin. Thick dark liquid sprayed out from Julian's direction and drenched her from head to toe.

"Julian," she hissed. "What in the stars were you thinking?" She stared at the oil splattered across the floor, recoiling as it stuck to her clothes and in her bangs.

Julian scowled back. He stood by one of the individual aquarium's filters, wrench in hand. "The motor on the plankton tank was stuck, and I wasn't about to let them swim in filth all night."

The plankton tank did seem murkier than the others. The luminescent creatures were much larger than their earthly counterparts but would still fit in the palm of Nadia's hand.

Nadia gestured to the massive oil spill on the floor. "We were done," she said. "Couldn't you have asked for help after we left?"

Julian tightened something inside the motor and shut the lid. "Why would I do that when I can fix it myself?"

"Except you clearly couldn't, because you made a mess." Nadia grabbed the mop off its hanger and thrust it into Julian's hands. "Here. Good luck getting it off the floor."

She stomped back to the supply closet and refilled the bucket with grease-resistant soap and water, trying not to breathe in the overwhelming smell of oil.

It was just like Julian to try to fix something and damage her in the process.

Scrubbing at the glass took twice as long as before as she struggled to remove the oil. Her anger at Julian bubbled under the surface.

Finally, the floors once again glistened. Nadia threw the rag she used in the trash instead of the laundry and headed toward the door, ready to shower off the putrid scent. Julian trudged behind.

Nadia pressed down the on red button to open the doors and nothing happened.

The doors were locked.

Nadia's heart froze. She pressed the red button faster, pushing repeatedly to no avail.

"We're too late." Julian arrived behind her, breathless. "The doors automatically lock for civilians after twenty-three hundred hours."

A dim memory of these rules lit in Nadia's brain. In order to keep the animals secure, the aquarium locked after a certain time and could only be opened with a special keycard.

"We can't be too late. I will not be locked in here all night with—" she cut off, staring forlornly at the seal between the doors.

"With me," finished Julian. He dropped the bucket and slumped against the nearest wall, facing the dragonshark exhibit. The single scaly inhabitant swam near the glass, smoke nonexistent in the depths of its tank.

Nadia gathered her hair and held it off her neck as claustrophobia settled in with the weight of being locked inside. She looked anxiously at her watch.

Six hours. Double the amount of time Nadia and Julian were scheduled to be in the aquarium. The doors would open at five when the first keepers came in to check on the early risers.

Nadia suppressed all of the snippy comments that came to mind and focused on slowing her breathing. She refused to look at Julian.

"I, under no circumstances, meant for this to happen," he said.

She ignored him, instead watching in silence as the green-scaled sirenshark swished in her soundproof tank. The sirenshark was best known for luring in its prey with a low whine, and humans were no exception. Any keeper who worked with the sirensharks wore earplugs.

"Nadia," said Julian, panic filling his voice. Nadia didn't reply. "Oriole's stuck." He knew all of her nicknames for the animals.

She turned and saw the orange crescent moon creeper with a tentacle wedged firmly under the large rock in his exhibit. Her heart beat faster as she took in the situation. Unlike other tentacled creatures, crescent moon creepers didn't regenerate lost limbs. Once it was gone, it would be gone forever. Oriole had already lost one tentacle prior to boarding the spaceship. To lose another would severely limit his movement.

Typically, crises were handled by an overnight keeper monitoring the exhibits from a remote location. With the lights still on in the aquarium signaling Nadia and Julian's presence, she doubted anyone would be coming for help. It was up to them to make sure the animals stayed healthy till the morning.

"One of us has to free him," she said. Any qualms she had with Julian became void when an animal was in trouble. They had taken a scuba certification class together in order to study the aquarium wildlife up close and help with habitat upkeep. Most exhibits could fit several people at once and still leave room for the creature inside.

Realization dawned on her. "I can't go," said Nadia. She picked at her shirt, where the oil from the filter motor had dried. She didn't want the oil in her hair mixing with the water.

"I guess that means it's up to me," Julian said. He suited up quickly, using one of the wetsuits stored in the aquarium. Nadia helped strap the air tank to him and checked to make sure everything was secure, keeping a close eye on Oriole's tentacle. It remained securely wedged underneath the rock.

"You're good," said Nadia, pulling firmly on the strap one last time. Julian disappeared for a moment behind the exhibit, where a ladder marked by chipped paint led to a small metal hatch. The hatch opened a foot above the water, allowing divers to enter without disrupting wildlife. Nadia listened the groan of the hatch as it twisted open.

Julian reappeared inside the tank, swimming toward Oriole. He gently pushed against the rock until it lifted. Oriole snatched his tentacle back and moved away from Julian.

Oriole didn't seem to be bleeding. He moved into the seagrass area of his tank and disappeared between the green leaves.

Julian grinned at her from inside the tank, eyes alight. Nadia found herself smiling at his back as he swam back toward the hatch and exited the tank.

Julian dripped water onto the floor as he moved away from the exhibit, shaking droplets from his hair. His grin didn't fade when he approached. "I will never get tired of that."

Nadia looked down at her oil-covered shoes. Adrenaline rushed over her, realizing how special it was to take care of the wildlife around them. It was something she and Julian still bonded over. No amount of discord between them could change that.

A faint crack resounded in the silence. Nadia looked around, examining the nearby tanks for any fractures in the glass. She peered into the stardust sea turtle tank and gasped. One of the shells had split, a tiny turtle poking its head out of the sand. Like all baby sea turtles, he appeared to be dusted in gold.

"Julian," she whispered. "The stardusts are hatching."

He stood next to her, looking in at the little turtle as it struggled out of the soft eggshell. Nadia didn't have her tablet, so she pulled a pen from her back pocket and scribbled the turtle number on her hand. It would be important when the keepers came back in the morning.

She settled in next to the tank, watching as another turtle pushed out of its egg and scrambled through the sand. In this artificial environment, there were no predators keeping the baby turtles from reaching the water. The tiny reptiles looked like specks of light as they crawled.

Julian sat next to her, a few feet apart. In the quiet of the moment, she didn't protest. Calm settled over her as she watched new life move to safety.

They stayed silent, Nadia marking down each new sea turtle as they hatched.

Lights in the aquarium dimmed from lack of movement. Neon stars stuck on the cavernous ceiling glowed to life one by one, softly illuminating the tanks.

"We live in space," whispered Julian softly. "Why use artificial constellations?"

Nadia regarded the mismatched stars. None of them reflected the true celestial pattern that surrounded their ship, instead mapping new shapes and constellations.

"I think there's something poetic about it," she said. "Even in the midst of all that's around us, we're still trying to create something beautiful and new. We aren't limited by the stars but by our own imaginations." She paused, studying a constellation in the shape of a bird with a top hat. "Or maybe it's meaningless."

Julian stared at her with those soft eyes, and Nadia was taken back to the night six months ago when he'd boarded a space pod headed toward Earth, ready to leave her and the star cruiser behind. Her chest ached with a twinge of the hurt and anger she had felt when she learned that he planned to leave without notice, without saying goodbye. The knowledge that even though the space pod malfunctioned, and he had to stay, their relationship was effectively ruined.

Nadia and Julian had argued their way through the whole scenario time and again. There was nothing left to discuss, no loose ends to resolve.

"Look, do you think we could ever be…" he trailed off, staring up at the fabricated constellations on the ceiling. If Nadia squinted enough, she could almost picture them being real. "I'm not talking about friends, Nadia. Just…not enemies."

Nadia let out a soft breath, staring intently at Blue the narwhal across the aisle. Blue stared back, his horn shimmering in front of him. A calm resolve settled in her stomach, and she tore her gaze away from the narwhal to look at Julian.

"I think it's possible," she said in little more than a whisper. "Some day."

He met her gaze. Inches and eons stretched between them.

Without warning, the doors slid open. Nadia and Julian sprang up from the floor by the sea turtle tank. The young keeper startled when she spotted them, and she almost dropped her evaluation tablet.

"My stars—what happened?"

"We got locked in," Nadia said with a yawn. She rubbed at her eyes. The tiredness was starting to set in, and she could imagine nothing more exciting than crawling into her bed for a long nap.

"The crescent moon creeper got stuck, but we freed him," said Julian. He tucked his hands into his pockets and yawned..

"And Henrietta's—the stardust sea turtle's—eggs started to hatch. We took note of the few that have braved the sand." Nadia showed the keeper the messy ink scratched on her hand.

The keeper studied Nadia and Julian with careful eyes. "Thank you for helping with that," she said. "Are you guys okay?"

Nadia looked at Julian, the animosity she'd once felt no longer burning in her chest. Instead of seeing a man who'd tried to leave her, she saw someone who had made a mistake and tried to atone. Someone to forgive.

"Yeah," she said, looking back at the keeper. "We're going to be okay."

A BREATH OF FRESH WATER

Sarah Calaway

I basically lived in the ocean. Or, rather, on top of it.

I lived on a large cruise ship that sailed ten out of months. In fact, I was pretty sure I was born on that ship. After all, my parents refused to leave their baby—their money maker—for anything. My birth wasn't even important enough for them to give up their love of money. I'd like to say it was because of their love of the sea, but that simply wasn't true. My parents loved the money of the people who boarded their cruise ship. They loved it more than me. No, only *I* loved the sea. The sea was my only friend on that ship.

I digress. This particular day was bland, boring, nothing. The sky was a glimpse of gray, and the water rocked the ship aggressively. The wind whipped my hair, several strands getting caught in front of my eyes. Clouds seemed to dance in the sky as I watched them. It was a slow and steady dance, never ending, the white wisps never seeming to stop and think about where they were going or why. They just went peacefully along with the flow. I wished I could do that.

I sat on top of my chair, enjoying the sound of the waves. I loved the sound of the seagulls, the laughter of the children, and the roar of the wind. These sounds were familiar to me, soothing even. I allowed myself to smile for a moment before turning back to the book in my hands and flipping the page while my mother worked on some mindless chore next to the railing. If she were to ask for my opinion, which she never did, I would wonder why she was so close to the rusting metal barely providing a barrier between her body and the vast sea below.

"Jasmina!" Dad huffed, storming over to me and pointing to my mother, her hands clenching the guard rail. Her face was pale as snow, body hunched over the side of the ship. She was half on the ship, half over the open sea.

"Yes?" I asked politely, setting the book in my lap and marking my page with the tip of my finger.

"Why aren't you helping your mother?"

I laughed bitterly, pointing to the oxygen tank by my side, then to the tubing snaking up to my nostrils. "Why don't you be useful for once and help her?"

His face turned red. "Why must you talk to me that way? It's every day with your attitude, Jasmina."

I rolled my eyes and reopened my book. Most would think of me as an ungrateful child. They would think that I was rude and uneducated in the proper way to talk to my elders. The truth was, it did not matter to me anymore. They treated me like an object, like a disposable employee instead of a daughter. Instead of paying for treatments for my lungs, they spent their money on booze and gambling. They would then yell at me, blaming me for their financial deficit when I never asked to be born, nor to be sick. They made me work on their cruise ship to earn back the meager money they paid for my treatments. By meager, I meant that they only paid for oxygen and yearly check ups. They wouldn't even put me on the transplant list. That would cost too much for an organ that would surely fail me again, they said.

Dad gave up on speaking to me when a few customers walked onto the deck, probably hoping to use the small pool in the center. Most patrons were inside due to the inclement weather and raindrops threatening to fall. However, my dad had to keep up his nice guy image, even if it were just two passengers. Even just one. Because they needed to come back, he said. They needed to feel like we were a family-run business.

Eventually, my parents walked inside to the bar area as rain began to fall from the sky. The fat drops landed all over my nose, glasses, and book. I tried to shield the book with my frail body, but it was no use. The wind whipped the droplets in every direction, causing the pages to turn all by themselves. With a long sigh, I placed my actual bookmark, a flattened seashell, inside the pages, and started my slow walk inside. One hand clutched the book to my chest, the other wheeled the oxygen tank. I almost lost my balance a few times as the ship was battered by the storm, but I finally made it inside.

The bar bustled with activity. Jerry, the new bartender, was busy serving cocktails and beers to a crowd around his counter. I liked him better than the old bartender because he snuck me a few cocktails even though I was only seventeen, which was too young to drink in most waters we traveled. I think he felt pity towards me because I was dying. I didn't have to tell him; everyone could see it. The sunken eyes, my ribs poking out, my inability to walk very far even with the oxygen tank. I usually hated pity, but I loved when it got me things I couldn't normally have.

Today, I sat at the bar with Jerry. An older lady offered me her seat. I was too exhausted from my short walk to refuse. I just wanted water, I told him. He obliged, and I sat on the stool staring at the bar that had been empty for the last year and a half. Now, it was bustling with life.

Business sucked for my parents. There was no sugar coating it. They barely had thirty people—if even that— on their cruises. They tried raising the prices to make ends meet, but it didn't work. So they tried lowering the prices so more people would find it affordable and book a trip, but that didn't work either.

As morbid as it sounds, the only thing that worked was Emily. Mom's best friend passed away from cancer a few months ago, and she made Mom promise to adopt Emily in the event she passed. Emily's mom was a single mother, and we were the only other family she had. In fact, Emily and I had grown up as sisters. I was her big sister, and she doted on me. She looked up to me, and it was funny because I had started to resent her. Of course,

I hadn't started to resent her until after the adoption went through. She was a sweet, cute little girl, but my parents loved her more than me. It was only a matter of time before they saw her as nothing more than a dollar sign, just like me.

Emily walked into the bar then, and all eyes turned to her. People now saw us as a loving family taking in a grief-stricken girl. They saw us trying to give her the best life possible: a fun, happy life. All the funds from this cruise trip were supposed to go to her mom's memorial fund, which was supposed to go to cancer research. I could tell right then that was false, and every cent would go in my parents' pockets to fuel their addictions of alcohol and gambling. Emily was just an excuse to boost their business, and I wish she had gone to some other family who would actually love her. Foster care would have been better than my parents' care. Because if she ever got sick, if she ever had expensive medical bills like me, she would be blamed for it for the rest of her life, just like me.

My parents walked over to her, probably to guide her out of the bar. A seven-year-old in a crowded bar full of drunk idiots would not make them look like good parents. Emily's eyes scanned the room, and they met mine. Her eyes were vibrant blue, like the ocean of the Caribbean. They were the opposite of mine, which were muddy and brown. Her hair was also the opposite of mine, meaning it was a blonde that shone gold like the sun.

I knew she felt scared and out of place. Even after seventeen years of living on that stupid ship, I felt out of place. However, I couldn't make myself go over to her and grab her hand to comfort her. I was a jerk like that. I knew it was selfish and cruel, and I knew it wasn't her fault that my parents were using her for their own gain. I just couldn't help feeling betrayed. I just didn't understand the plan of putting her into my life to ruin hers and mine at the same time. My parents were cruel, heartless people, and I didn't understand why they got to have the perfect life. Well, it wasn't like I was a child anymore. In a few months, I could legally move out into a house on my own. But I would probably be dead by then, or not at all in the shape to work to make money for myself. My parents definitely wouldn't support me. After all, when we didn't live on that cruise ship, we lived in a terribly run-down apartment just off of 2nd Street in a small city named Robstown.

I looked up, snapping out of my thoughts. My parents must have led Emily away, because she wasn't there anymore. I breathed a sigh of relief, but it was more like a cough because my lungs were failing again; it was starting to hurt to breathe. Or maybe it was because of the anxiety disorder that I knew I had, but my parents wouldn't bother to have me checked for. I placed my head down against the counter, and I knew it was dirty, but I didn't care. I needed to drown out all the noise. I needed to control my breathing, because my lungs were inefficient as it was. I couldn't breathe, I couldn't think, all I could see in my closed eyes was Emily's innocent little face. I could think of her getting yelled at for being born, crying in her bedroom late at night, wondering why her parents had even bothered to have a child at all. I knew that her mom had actually wanted her and would have gone to the ends of the Earth to protect her and tell her that she was loved, but she wasn't here anymore. In fact, her mom was more of a mom to me than my own mother ever was, and that was the saddest fact of all. I didn't know how Aunt Jennifer could have been friends with a sadistic creature like my mother.

I must have fallen asleep, even with all the noise. When I awoke, the bar was empty, and night had fallen. I walked out of the bar and onto the deck. Artificial lights shone down on the pool, which was full of people. The wooden deck was still stained with rain, but the night sky had cleared up enough to show the twinkling stars. It was actually quite a beautiful sight, and I went back to my chair by the side of the railing. I knew my parents wanted me to work, but I just couldn't do it. My health wasn't up to it, and I didn't care what they thought anymore.

I realized I forgot my book as I looked down at my empty hands, so I stared out at the pool, lights twinkling. I wished they would just shut off all the artificial light so that I could just look at the stars in all their magnificence. They reminded me of myself, seeming small and miniscule, their real beauty observed when all the lights were off, and not everyone was watching.

I decided to glance around, and Emily was running around with a little boy I didn't recognize. He must have been a few years younger than her, maybe five or six years of age. He reminded me of a boy that I used to see in the ocean swimming next to the cruise ship. He had a tail with pretty scales, and I was pretty sure I imagined him. Yet, I saw him every day until I was eleven years old, and then he stopped coming by. It really hurt my feelings, considering he was really my only friend.

Emily walked over to me, and I tried to look anywhere but at her.

"Will you come play with us, Jasmina?" she asked, a hopeful look in her eyes.

I shook my head. "Leave me alone."

She pouted. "Pretty please?"

"I said no, you brat!" I hissed, and I regretted it as soon as I said it.

The light left her eyes. The boy, upset, tried to grab my arm.

I pulled back.

Emily grabbed my other arm, attempting to pull me out of my chair.

"Come on!" Emily cried. "You never play with me!"

The tug-of-war probably lasted for a few seconds before inertia took over, and I found my body flying against the railing. Only, the ship hadn't been serviced properly in years, and the railing was rusted, so it gave way.

It was a shock when my body hit the cold water. I gasped for air, and I realized my oxygen tank hadn't come with me. The tubing must have gotten caught on something and ripped away from my nostrils.

I knew I couldn't last long with my lungs, and I didn't have the strength to swim or fight. I sank pretty quickly, and not even a cry of help escaped me. I couldn't breathe; my vision went black. It felt like air had been replaced with water rather quickly inside my lungs, almost like the feeling of accidentally having water go down the wrong way. I felt this strong urge to cough, to rid my lungs of this new feeling, this intruder. I had no fight in me, but it was okay. I was going to die soon anyway, and I would rather die in something I loved than up on the deck with my parents.

I said a prayer. I said a prayer because I was scared, and wherever I went, I hoped it would be heaven. I believed that it would be heaven, but maybe with the way I treated Emily it would be hell.

The last thing I expected to was a dark blob, floating. Was it floating towards me, or was it just a blur of my vision? I blinked, and the salt water stung my eyes. I would have figured someone jumped in to save me, but there had been no splash, just someone swimming next to me as if they had already been in the water.

Arms wrapped around my torso and dragged me deeper into the water. I panicked only for a second, but I knew I was going to die either way. I was probably hallucinating at this point anyway.

"Jas!" I heard a familiar voice call. "Jas, can you hear me?"

Everything was muffled, but this voice rang out above the thoughts clouding my mind. In my oxygen-deprived state, it was difficult to remember where I had heard the voice before. My chest fluttered to hear that voice, and I longed to put a face and name to it, but I couldn't see anything. I could only hear voices that slowly became disoriented, and I could feel arms tightening around me. I was panicking, hyperventilating, letting more and more water into my lungs until I felt nothing and was nothing.

I awoke with a gasp, voices quieting around me. I couldn't make out any of the voices, and my eyes fluttered before opening fully. My whole body felt like something had changed drastically, but my brain couldn't pinpoint the difference quite yet.

"I think she's waking up," a voice said.

The air didn't feel right. It didn't feel like air. Oxygen. Where was my oxygen tank? I reached out my hand, trying to grab my tank. I didn't even feel the tubing in my nose. I needed that tank. I wouldn't survive without it. Not with the condition my lungs were in. Yet my lungs didn't burn. My lungs felt weird yet perfect. I felt like I was actually taking in one hundred percent of the air around me, even without my oxygen tank.

My eyes adjusted, and I was surrounded by people. I lay on a makeshift sort of bed, but my arms and legs were loosely strapped down. I could still move my arms around, so it wasn't exactly an effective restraint. I panicked, trying to sit up, but I couldn't.

"Stop. Ma'am, I need you to calm down. I—"

"Jasmina," another voice said.

"What?"

"That's her name. Jasmina. And she's probably terrified right now. Let me do the talking, please. I need this room clear."

Blurry shapes came into focus as everyone left. All but one. His face came into view as he came closer. He had such a familiar face, a familiar smile. I remembered that crooked nose, lopsided smile, but it couldn't be. It wasn't possible. If it was actually him, then I was dead, because he couldn't be real.

"Jas," he smiled. "It's been a long time."

"Jack," I breathed. "You're not real. You're imaginary. Am I losing my mind?" I tried again to free myself from the restraints on my limbs.

His tail was just like I remembered. "Relax. The restraints are to prevent you from floating upwards until you get used to…conditions down here."

"Down where?" I looked around. I was underwater. All my movements felt exaggerated. How was I breathing? If my lungs were terrible above water, there was no way I should've been alive under it.

"Jas, I am real. I know this is going to be scary to hear. I know that you're terrified right now, but it's okay. You're okay. You're safe here. And honestly, I missed you. You were my best friend, even though everyone made fun of me for befriending a random girl on a cruise ship." He smiled that same lopsided smile I remembered from his face as a child. He was actually quite handsome: dark hair, honey-brown eyes, dark complexion.

I laughed, laughed like I had lost my mind. I had figured that I was either dead or crazy at this point anyway. How was I alive underwater talking to my childhood imaginary friend who was a merman?

But I had laughed without pain—without gasping for air—in so long. It felt so good. Even if I was laughing because I thought I was delirious, it felt oddly nice.

"Calm down. I need you to calm down a little. You're going to break yourself out," he said. His voice sounded the exact same as it did when he was younger—when I imagined him younger.

"I'll calm down when I figure out what's going on and why I've lost my mind!" I tried to get up again, but he gently placed a hand on my arm. He felt so real. His touch felt so real, like he was really next to me, talking to me, reassuring me.

"I need you to give me a few minutes to explain. I need you to listen, to not interrupt, to not freak out. If you still need more information or think that you're crazy, which you're not, then I'll give you the time that you need. Nod if you understand."

I slowly nodded; I needed something to still my racing heart and spinning thoughts. Maybe my brain would explain to me whatever it wanted for me to register. Maybe a real doctor was talking to me, but some wires got crossed and I was imagining them as my imaginary friend. I was truly terrified of whatever came next, but no matter how much I hyperventilated from panic, my lungs felt better than they had in years. I didn't understand.

The last thing I remembered was drowning. I fell off the cruise ship because Emily wanted to play. Emily. Emily was all alone with my parents, and the last thing I said to her was insulting her, calling her a brat. I was mean to her, but I still cared. I missed her.

"Can I start, please?"

I gave him a thumbs up. I had to be ready.

"You see, mermaids are real. We're clever, we're a highly evolved species." He stopped and chuckled to himself. "I mean, we're not all great. But we definitely exist. We just don't like for humans to bother us. But we've mingled with humans more than we care to admit. That's why many of us can speak English on this side of the world, why we have technology so close to your kind. However, ours is a bit more advanced. For example, we were able to cure your lungs. Humans couldn't have done that without a transplant, but even that is not really a cure. However, your lungs are only cured underwater. I know you always talked about how much you hated your parents and your life. I'm not sure if you have anything to go back to, and trust me, I didn't want to take away your option. You would've drowned if we didn't act. There was no way to get you back on board the ship on time, not with your lungs the way they were."

I stared at him for a moment. "The only person I would go back for is my sister."

He blinked, confused. "I never realized you had a sister."

"She's not my biological sister. I just…. I blamed her for things that were not her fault at all. And now she's alone with my terrible, manipulative parents." Could I cry underwater? I wanted to cry.

"Jas, I'm so sorry. I'm sorry I stopped seeing you. Just like humans try to convince each other that we are a myth, we convince our offspring that humans are a myth. I listened to them for so long, and then I couldn't find your ship." He took a long, deep breath. "I missed you."

"I missed you too," I whispered. "But I still think I'm crazy. It's just hard to believe my lungs could be cured, or that any of this actually exists." I looked around the room. It looked like it had white walls, but it was different from a normal room on land. It looked almost made of glass and painted over. The room had so much technology that was foreign to me. Nothing felt real. Nothing was familiar.

He grabbed my hand and held it firmly. His skin felt a bit more slimy than my own, almost like fish scales that looked like my skin. "I need you to understand that it'll be a difficult change, and not everyone will accept you here. But you'll have the best care here, I'll make sure of it. And I'll always be here if you need me."

I smiled. "Even if I am crazy, I guess I'll have to adjust to whatever reality this is." I squeezed his hand. We had never made physical contact before, which helped me believe he was just a figment of my imagination. But now, he was really here in front of me. We were really under the ocean, or maybe not. It didn't matter. Jack wanted what was best for me. He was my best friend as a child and I missed him, but he was back. My lungs were finally cured. I was no longer the sick girl that everyone pitied. I just missed Emily. If I had Emily with me, wherever I was, I could be happy.

"We are decently peaceful right now, however—"

Suddenly, the room had another individual.

"Jackson, they need you. And it's time for me to do a full workup on the, um, patient," a merman in a white coat stated. He looked like he hated me.

They began speaking in a language I couldn't understand. I felt a bit panicked again as Jack left my side. He smiled and said something else, but I was already losing consciousness, but I couldn't pinpoint why, maybe panic, maybe something medical, maybe just because.

"You're only the leader because your parents are dead, Jackson. They would not be happy that you brought a human into everything they've built. Especially not *their* child. The offspring of those imbeciles!"

"She hates them! They let her rot!" Jack yelled. "And if you don't want to continue taking care of her, that's fine. I'll find someone else who cares to listen to authority!"

The other voice was silent for a few moments. "Fine. But I want a raise."

"Whatever, it'll be discussed."

I felt a hand on my arm. "Jas, hey."

My eyes slowly opened. It took a few moments to adjust to the room. "Hi, Jack."

"You should be well enough to leave this room soon. I'll get a place for you to stay."

"What did they mean, 'especially not *their* child?'" I asked. "Why do they all seem to hate me? I don't remember doing anything."

He shook his head. "It's complicated. Really, uh, complicated. I don't want to get into it right now."

"I'm stuck in this room not knowing anyone but you. My whole life has been thrown upside down. Please. I need to know everything."

He sighed, avoiding eye contact. His hand dropped from my arm, and his shoulders drooped, eyes downcast. "Your parents are not good people. Not at all. They—to keep their business afloat, to keep themselves rich and healthy, they made a deal with people they shouldn't have. They're notorious down here. I really shouldn't talk about this right now. Not while you're recovering."

I reached out for his hand again, He pulled away, turned to face the weird wall they had in the weird room. Everything just felt so weird to me. I still couldn't believe I was underwater. I still believed I was crazy, but this was so oddly specific and consistent.

"Jack, just tell me. I'm used to hearing bad news. It's literally my whole life."

"Jasmina," he started, faltering on his words. "I can't. I can't."

"You can. I deserve to know, right? It's my parents."

He sat on the edge of my bed, still facing away from me. "There are different groups of us based on the region of the world. This group, well, my parents were the leaders. They were, well, they, um, passed. Long story short, I'm in charge now, but there's a group that's broken off from us. The best English translation is 'The Traitors'. They hate the humans enough to experiment on them, torture them. Even torture their own kind for more technology, more money, to make a point."

"That's terrible," I said flatly. I couldn't process emotion.

He nodded. "Your parents made a deal with them. Each cruise, they provide people that won't be missed. They make sacrifices. Human sacrifices. And The Traitors give them technology, wealth, whatever else they made a deal with. Your parents are very well known under water. But I've always known you couldn't be a part of it. The look on your face right now tells me that I've been right all along."

It felt like the whole world was caving in around me, trying to suffocate me. Maybe I couldn't breathe underwater anymore. There was no way. No. They couldn't have been involved in all this. This didn't make sense. It couldn't exist. None of this was real. Was it? No. No. No.

"I'm sorry. I knew it was too much! Jas? J—"

"I need to fix this! How do we take them down? How do we stop it? Tell me!" I screamed, taking him by surprise. The tears from my eyes mingled with the water already surrounding me. It all felt so surreal.

"No. You cannot be involved. You—"

"I need to. You don't understand, I haven't done anything in seventeen years. I feel like a waste of space. I need to stop my parents, and I need to save my sister. Can we do that? Is it possible?"

"It's possible, but it will take a lot of planning and consideration."

"I don't care. Let's do it."

It took me months to properly train. Training involved learning how to move underwater, how to get used to my improved lungs, and how to protect myself. Jack was very reluctant to teach me how to fight, but I wanted to. I needed to. And during all this, he provided me space in his own home to stay. It took a while to learn how to not float to the top of the enclosure while sleeping, but my body got used to this new sense of gravity.

According to the calendar on the wall, it had been three months since I almost met my demise. Three months since I lain in an underwater hospital and learned my childhood 'imaginary' friend was actually real.

Jack knocked, then swam through the doorway to my room.

I sat on my underwater version of a bed, staring at the wall made of one-way glass; I could see out, but no one could see in.

I opened my mouth to speak, but the look on his face made me close it. His face was grave. Had someone else died to The Traitors?

"Jas, I need to tell you something," he said, looking anywhere but at me. "You're going to be upset, but I need you to promise me that you won't do anything rash."

"Okay."

"The Traitors—"

"Let me guess, who did they kill this time?" I asked.

"They didn't kill anyone else. Yet."

I stood, making my way towards him. I still hated how the water slowed my movement. "Then what?"

He still couldn't look at me. "Jas, please. I'm begging you to let me handle this before I tell you."

"Well, if you would just tell me—"

"They have your sister. Emily."

My heart dropped. My mouth went dry, my heart hammered inside my chest, and I felt the sudden urge to vomit. "No. No, they can't. My parents wouldn't sacrifice her; she's their selling point, the money maker. She's just a child! They wouldn't." I wrapped my arms around myself, squeezing my eyes shut.

"They didn't. They stopped helping The Traitors and this was payback."

"No!" I screamed. "No, I refuse to believe that my parents would let them just take her. "

"They do. I'm sorry."

I opened my eyes. "Look at me. Look at me and tell me how we fix this."

"We can't. Not right now. I don't have the troops."

"That's my sister! My sister who I was terrible to because my life sucked. I need to make it up to her! I have to save her, one way or another! Im ready, whatever it takes."

He finally looked at me, pleading with his eyes. "Jasmina, give me time. I don't want anyone to get hurt, but we can't go into enemy territory without enough troops. That's a death wish. Give me time."

I was shaking. "How long?"

"A week. I'll call in the emergency troops, do what I can."

"A week?" I laughed. "A week? You think she has a week? A week in the hands of monsters?

He swam towards me, placing his scaly hands on my shoulders. "You're also human. It's a risk for you to come with me, but I'll allow it. However, I need more backup. We can't go on a suicide mission."

"Yes, I can. I'll do it for Emily, to undo what my parents have done. Get me who you can, or I leave without you."

"You don't even know where they are!"

I smirked. "You think I haven't spent the last three months in research? You think they keep their location very secret? If my parents could contact them, then so can I. I will not let them torture her."

He shook his head. "Fine. I'll get who I can, but that means it's too dangerous for you to come."

"Wrong."

"Just give me a little time," he said before he left the room.

How could I give him time when Emily was probably hurting, scared, and alone?

We left early the next morning. Sunlight hadn't warmed up the water yet, which was one thing I didn't think I'd ever get used to. The merpeople had these machines similar to human cars, but they were able to propel forward under water. The ride wasn't long at all, but my stomach was a pit of nerves. I had no idea what to expect when it came to saving Emily. I didn't even know if Emily could be saved. I hoped she could. I hoped she wasn't already gone.

There were about five underwater vehicles that carried six people each. There were only thirty of us willing to take back my sister. I all but cried the whole way into enemy territory while everyone around me spoke in a language I couldn't understand. It was terrifying knowing I had to wait hours, not knowing if this would even work. I hoped it worked. I really needed her to be safe.

When the vehicle stopped, I froze. It was oddly quiet. Then the shots rang out. Mermaid soldiers left their vehicles to fire weapons oddly similar to guns on land, but something seemed different. You could see the ammunition barreling towards the enemy, disturbing the water around it. Through this chaos, Jack got into the front seat with the controls. We were the only ones left in the vehicle. I was thrown back against the seat as he pressed a lot of buttons and we were barreling straight towards the enemy gates, which were locked tight.

I screamed as it sounded like metal fought metal. Something hit us and we launched sideways, spun, and then I was upside down, screaming.

"Jack!" I called. "Are you okay?"

No response. I managed to wrestle with the door and climb out. I was bleeding from somewhere, maybe my head. Crimson stained the watter above me. I reached for the small weapon Jack gave me that I stuffed into the waistband of my pants.

"Freeze!"

I spun around and pressed the trigger button. *Boom!* The merman was blown away from me, shouting the whole way. I trembled, trying to keep my balance under water.

"Jack?"

I tried to reach the driver's side, but it was smashed in. I started swimming as fast as I could to the building Jack had shown me on the blueprint. If I could get Emily, then I could help Jack. I just had to get to my sister first.

The building was huge and painted black, unusual for structures down below the surface. The guards had left to investigate the commotion.

I tried to slide the glass doors open. No such luck; it was locked. I stumbled backwards, aimed my weapon, and fired. Glass exploded, and I swam through it as fragments tore at my flesh.

"Emily!" I screamed. I looked around. The room was full of large, glass containers containing orangeish gooey liquid and humans. There were so many bodies. And smack in the middle was Emily.

I ran towards her, pressing my hands on the glass, pounding on it. "Emily! Can you hear me?" I prepared to aim my weapon at the lower end of the glass. I had to break her out.

I felt a hand on my shoulder. I jumped, spinning around to defend myself. It was Jack, a gash on his forehead and a somber look on his face.

"She's gone."

"No!" I shouted, turning back to the glass. Her eyes were closed, and she looked almost peaceful. "No. We can get her out. I'm sure she's just suspended somehow. Isn't that how this stupid technology works?"

"No. Once she's in orange, it's too late. They're just saving her body, but her spirit is long gone. I'm sorry."

"No," I repeated numbly. My body tried to sink to the ground, like it could no longer support my weight, but instead I just floated there, knees bent, eyes unable to blink, to tear away from the sight in front of me.

"Let's get you out of here."

A year. It had been a year since I found out my sister died for my parents' crimes. The Traitors had mostly been taken down, but a lot of Jack's men went with them. I hadn't been to the surface in a year and three months, but it was time.

I hadn't told Jack. He was my best friend, like a brother I never had. He wouldn't agree with what I was doing. In fact, he told me that breathing air again could undo the science that kept me alive and breathing underwater. I no longer cared.

It took a while to get to the surface. It wasn't that the mermaid society was extremely deep, it was just that I had spent way too long trying to keep myself under water that my whole sense of gravity had changed. It probably took hours, maybe even days, of swimming, relaxing, swimming again before I spotted the cruise ship. It looked huge from this angle.

Once my head broke the surface, I knew I wouldn't have much time. I had to act fast. I took in one last breath of ocean water before springing to the surface. I was able to grab onto the railing and quickly pull myself up. I had oddly gained strength while under water. The air burned my skin, as did the bright sun beating down on me. Mother was on the deck as she usually was this time of day, talking to guests.

Her gaze traveled in my direction and she jumped. I charged towards her. My lungs burned; I was surprised my legs worked on land. Maybe it was the mermaid science keeping me strong, maybe it was adrenaline.

"Jasmina? No. No, you drowned! Help!" Mother screamed.

I was right in front of her. I let out the breath I had taken in. Water dribbled out from my mouth. "Where— Dad?" I stuttered.

"No. He's dead, and you're dead, and—"

Dad was dead? He deserved it. I just wished he had been there for my plan.

I was feeling faint. My lungs burned. I could feel my body shutting down. With my last bit of strength, I charged at her, pushing her over the railing. I clung to her as we both hit the water.

"This is for Emily." I said.

It was the last thing I ever said.

A SEA FULL OF STARS

A Nathal Short Story

Anne J. Hill

The deck is bare of human life other than the pirate pacing and watchkeeping. Only the moon and stars keep him company this night.

The watchkeeper's boots clip across the swaying deck. His hands are clasped behind his back, head tilted high. Waves lap against the side of the ship and rock him to an unheard lullaby. The air tastes far too familiar tonight. Like an old memory personally sent from the ocean to his lips.

It's been years since he got his sea legs, but this feels as though it's his first time traveling the ocean.

Alone. With the stars and moon.

This rugged ship has been through too much in her time, making each footstep creak out in weary pain. The watchkeeper has never bonded with this vessel nor with the rest of her crew, and guilt rides over him like an unwanted love affair. He's only recently boarded her after the unfortunate events of his past ship. The one he captained and loved selflessly for years—*The Howler.*

Captains are meant to go down with their ships.

He'd jumped his ship. A lover leaving his darling to sink alone in a sea full of death.

And now he stands alone on unfamiliar wood with a crew that isn't his. When he was captain, he would have never been caught pacing the decks in the dead of night. That is not a captain's duty. Not in his mind.

He takes in a sharp breath and swallows it. All he has to do is keep breathing. And for now, pacing. Ignoring the thoughts playing over in his head. The ones that have haunted him for years. Nothing else will pass the time during this night shift.

A good captain always goes down with his ship. If you can find a good captain, he'll strap himself to the mast and dive to the depths with his vessel.

A cloud glides over the moon, stealing his main source of light. A shiver wafts through the air at the memories.

A good captain wouldn't be ghostly white and praying to be saved. He'd sink, willingly, with a smile.

His feet refuse to pace anymore, and his hands grip the railing. His toes push up so he can lean over and stare the lethal waves in the face. Images of *The Howler* sinking as he stood safely on an island—half his crew panting on the shoreline—course through his mind. The screaming, the fire, the cannonballs.

He'd fled like the least of them and did nothing to save the rest of his crew or his beautiful vessel.

But now is his chance to join them as he floats over the very spot where *The Howler* once sank.

He teeters over the rail and flirts with death like she is his new lover. Mist sprays his face, promising instant relief if he simply jumps into the sea's warm embrace.

Something stirs in the water. Something other than the waves that smack the side of the ship.

"Jump. Join us," a voice whispers from the sea. A smiling woman slowly emerges, her expression assuring warmth and safety. Her fin gracefully flaps under the water.

He rubs his eyes, blinking at the mermaid. Never has he seen such a beautiful creature, black hair trickling down her bare chest and eyes the color of the sea. "Have I gone mad?" he whispers to the beauty.

The merwoman smiles. Her hand reaches up towards him. The ship shifts towards her, and she grabs the taffrail to pull herself up so they're face to face. She touches his cheek. She is flesh. She is real. Her fingers are smooth against his rough skin.

Knowing something so fantastical exists in his world almost makes him want to ground his feet to the deck and press on, but—

"Come, Silus," the mermaid whispers as she traces the line along his jaw. Water drizzles down her pale cheek and over her lips, and the urge to kiss those lips for an eternity knots itself in his stomach.

She knows his name.

A shiver runs down his spine, and he smiles. Many know his name, but none say it like they know *him*, know the horrors of his past and his choices. As if she can somehow read his soul at first glance.

"Follow me." She slips back into the water and lifts her hand to him. The waves tip the ship sideways so that if he leans out, he can entwine his fingers with hers.

"Yes," he whispers and reaches his hand towards death's open arms.

Jumping off a sinking ship is noble. Smart. Wise.

Abandon all hope, those who board.

Just one more shove, and he'll be consumed by the inviting depths.

Her fingers clasp around his, and he feels himself begin to slip over the edge, his feet coming off the deck.

The clouds part and something else in the dark water catches his eyes. A sparkle.

A star.

He tilts his head and gazes upward to find the moon and stars remaining strong. They dance and flicker—a reality worth living for.

He yanks his hand free of her grip. She seethes, fangs protruding as she lunges towards him. His feet hit solid wood, and the ship straightens to its full height. Her body slams against the ship's side.

He closes his eyes and takes a deep breath. One more step. One more day. He opens his eyes, and the siren is gone, washed away in the sea.

The sea that covers a multitude of sins.

The night slowly drifts away, and then dawn rises. The crew stirs; their voices chirp on deck. A hand lands on his shoulder with a welcoming squeeze, and the captain asks, "All good last night, sailor?"

Silus nods, a smile parting his lips. "All good, Captain."

"Couldn't have slept well without knowing you had your eye on things, Silus." The captain pats his back before turning away, adding, "Job well done."

A surge of renewed hope floods him. He can build a new life on this ship…

And Silus is no longer alone in the sea full of stars.

ADA

Shawn P B Robinson

Chapter One

I opened my eyes.

It took me a moment to make sense of what I saw. Squares. White… or off-white. I couldn't tell.

"Hello?"

A high voice. A woman's voice. I didn't know who she was talking to or where she was.

Movement to my right.

I turned my head, slowly at first. It was as if I didn't fully remember how to move my neck. As I turned, I caught on—the squares were ceiling tiles.

Her voice came again. "Hello?"

I focused on the woman. She wore white. Held a tube in her hand. One end ran to a bag, and the other ran down to my bed.

A nurse. I was in a hospital.

"Do you remember your name?"

Assess: She might not have clearance.
Decide: I have to maintain my cover.

"I don't remember."

She nodded. "That's understandable after all you've been through."

"What have I been through?"

She smiled at me. Her movements were off, her eyes a strange color. "I'll let the doctor bring you up to speed." A door opened, and she looked up. "Ah, perfect timing, Doctor."

I turned to see two men walk into the room. The one I didn't recognize. He was tall and thin, likely around thirty-five. The other man I knew well. I called him "Handler".

When Handler's eyes focused on me, he smiled. "Teran! It's good to see you awake. You've been out for days."

I flicked my eyes to the doctor and back to Handler.

Handler put his hands up and nodded. "It's okay, Teran. They both have full clearance for everything you have to say."

"What happened?" My mind was still a little sluggish. I only remembered bits and pieces of the mission. What I could remember was coming back slowly.

"That's a long story," Handler said as he put a hand on my left arm.

The pressure felt off. I could see his hand touching me, but something wasn't right.

Pain shot through my right arm, and I reacted without thought. I tried to pull away, but I couldn't move anything other than my neck.

"I'm sorry, sir," the doctor said, "we had to put you in restraints."

I tried to relax. The pain slowly eased off, but it had been enough to make me want to scream. "Why does my arm hurt so much?"

Handler gave the doctor a nod.

"Mr. Teran…" the Doctor began.

He didn't know my full name. Handler might believe the man had clearance, but the doctor didn't know everything. I'd need to keep some of my details close.

"You were in quite the accident," the Doctor continued. "When you came in, your right arm was severely damaged, along with your right shoulder and right kidney. A transport accident." He paused, and I suspected he was trying to give me a look of compassion. It didn't come naturally to him. "We had to replace the damaged tissue. Your arm, your shoulder, much of the muscle across your chest, all synthetic."

The thought that I'd lost my arm horrified me. I had heard about synthetic limbs, but I wasn't really familiar with them. People called them robot arms.

Trying to lighten the mood, I asked, "Does that mean I can punch through walls?"

"Perhaps," the doctor said with a frown.

No humor. I made a mental note not to joke around the man.

"You might also find that everything looks and feels a little off. Have you noticed that yet, Mr. Teran?"

I nodded. The movement felt strange, as if my brain shifted in a way it shouldn't.

"How did that movement feel, Mr. Teran? When you nodded your head, did it feel a little odd?"

"It did."

"Good," the doctor said. He turned to the nurse. "Release him from his restraints. He needs to move." To me, he added, "You suffered a concussion—a bad one. Everything's going to look and feel a little off for a time. We've fixed the concussion, just as we fixed your arm and shoulder, but it will take a few minutes to reorient yourself. The more you move, the more you will adjust to the new arm and the medication for your head. I expect if you do all your therapy, you should be back in the field within a day or two."

The doctor nodded to me and, without a word to Handler, left.

"Well, Mr. Teran, I bet it'll be nice to be out of these nasty restraints," the nurse said with a smile.

I took a deep breath the moment the steel chest strap released. My lungs felt strong and clear—almost healthier than they had in years.

A moment later, Handler was at my side, helping me into a seated position. "You have no idea how good it is to see you getting up, Teran. I've been so worried about you."

Handler and I had been friends for years. As far back as I could remember. He was always there. Even on many of my missions.

I slid off the bed, placing both feet on the ground. If Handler hadn't had his arm around me, and the nurse hadn't come in to help, I would have gone right down. The room spun, and I closed my eyes.

"No, Mr. Teran, open your eyes," the nurse said quickly. "You have to get used to everything, and you can't do that with your eyes closed."

I slowly reopened my eyes. My stomach twisted, my jaw did something funny. The floor seemed too far away.

I was a wreck.

I planted my feet firmly and balanced myself. My vision steadied. My hands stopped trembling.

"You're getting the hang of it, Mr. Teran. It doesn't take long. Everyone's always a little off after going through something like this."

"Going through something like what, exactly?"

"Trauma, Mr. Teran. With the loss of a limb and major organ, you're lucky we got to you so quickly."

The pain in my arm began to ease some more. I moved my shoulder. It felt awkward, but I felt strong. I couldn't help but think I really could punch through a wall.

"Let's go for a walk, Mr. Teran," the nurse said.

I took a step and found myself feeling much better. I put up my hand. "We'll be okay. You go back to what you need. If we need anything, I'll call you."

The nurse's piercing gaze bore into me as if she were trying to figure something out. A moment later, she nodded. "All right, Mr. Teran. If you need anything, just holler. You're the only patient on this floor. You won't disturb anyone else."

I moved toward the door with Handler. He'd always been my greatest support. Today was no different.

Once we were out of earshot, I asked once again, "How'd you come by that name?"

"My parents were odd," Handler explained. "They wanted to confuse me and everyone else."

I'd never heard that one before. Always a different answer.

"My mission?"

Handler nodded as we walked slowly down the hall. With every step, my balance improved. The colors were still wrong along with my depth perception, but I hoped it would all come back.

"You completed your mission," Handler said with a smile. "I don't know what all you remember from the last few hours before your accident, but we believe your infiltration was complete. All that's left is the debrief, and then we can take down Sigma."

I returned the smile. I couldn't quite remember how long I'd been undercover, but I had gained the trust of Marda—Sigma's leader—and had collected information on just about every terrorist cell around the world. We could finally end their influence, their violence, their lies.

We passed a porthole, and the sunlight shining through the ocean waters caught my eye. "I didn't realize we were this close to the surface. We're not in Havana anymore?"

Handler shook his head. "No, we're back in New Paris. The hospital is only about seventy feet below the surface."

New Paris. I'd only been there a few times. Sigma didn't have a cell in this city.

"Where's their main base of operations?" Handler asked.

"You don't want to wait for the debrief?"

He laughed. "No, I'm just curious. I thought perhaps Havana might be it, but many of the higher-ups thought it was likely one of the Asian cities."

"Both wrong. A lot of the action takes place in Havana, but Toronto is the place. Right down in the lower sections."

"I see. I look forward to—"

I hit the floor hard, chunks of the ceiling crashing down on me. I rolled and slammed up against the wall.

Assess: Not an accident—a bomb. Need to locate Handler.
Decide: Get up and get out.
Act: …

I pulled myself out from under the debris. An arm stuck out from under a few tiles, and I grabbed Handler and pulled him to his feet. He was dazed, but I didn't wait for him to focus. The chance of flooding was too great to remain near the site of the explosion.

I dragged him down the hallway, using my right arm to pull him along. It certainly did feel strong, and my balance had fully come back.

We were in a United World Network hospital— UnWoN—so it didn't surprise me to see the nurse step out from behind her counter with a pulse cannon.

Her job was to protect Handler and me.

And my job was to protect the information in my head.

Before we passed her position, she went down in a shower of bullets.

The enemy was inside.

I ran hard. At first, Handler stumbled along, but he slowly regained his footing. We'd be out soon.

I reached the door, but my body jerked to the side as something slammed into me. I rolled for a good ten feet or so, and sprung to my feet just as a second pulse blasted into me, slamming me up against the wall. Before I could get up, a bag came down over my head, and I felt restraints tighten around my wrists.

I couldn't see a thing through the bag. Multiple hands lifted me, and I heard the grunts. The quick glance I caught of them before they covered my face revealed six large men. Too many to take, even if I wasn't restrained.

I counted the hands holding me. At least ten, if not the full twelve. I hoped Handler survived. Maybe they left him behind.

Chapter Two

We moved through a series of doors, one of which had the familiar hiss of a port, and my footsteps on the metal floor had a unique ring to it. I'd recognize the sound of a subtrans anywhere.

We lurched away from the port, and the pressure in the subtrans increased. We were dropping toward the ocean floor.

"Do we take the bag off?"

I don't think the man who spoke intended for me to hear, but it was hard not to. He should learn to either send signals or whisper quietly enough that the target can't hear.

No response, just movement. The bag didn't come off, so I assumed the answer was a simple shake of the head.

"We've got company!"

I recognized that voice. Sted—a pilot. One of the best Sigma had. He was also one of their greatest strategists. They wouldn't risk him if they didn't think the mission was important.

Assess: Sigma has captured me. The restraints suggest that they suspect I'm their enemy, but the man's question about the bag suggests there is some doubt about my loyalties.

Decide: I must resume my mission to infiltrate Sigma until UnWoN can pull me out.

Act: …

"Wait," I called out, letting my voice sound weak and a little scratchy, "is that Sted? Who are you guys? You're…. Oh no, Sted! Have they captured you too?"

No response came, other than a sharp shift in the subtrans' movement. Sted needed to avoid whoever was tracking us. I gathered he wouldn't answer yet, but my question would continue to ring in their ears.

"Drop to the floor. We can lose them in the caves."

The man spoke with authority. I recognized his voice, but it was muffled. He likely had a mask on to disguise his face. That meant his identity was thought to be unknown to UnWoN.

Rick. Rick led this mission.

"Rick?" I asked, slipping just enough shock into my voice. "You're… wait… what's going on here, guys? I'm one of you! Why are you doing this to me?"

The subtrans lurched to the side, and the pressure regulators struggled. We were dropping fast.

"Teran," Rick said, "until we know for sure what's been done to you, our orders are to keep you restrained and keep the bag on your head."

The subtrans turned sharply once again. I figured Sted must have dodged something. Whatever it was, UnWoN wouldn't use torpedoes. They wanted me alive.

Captured by the enemy or not, at least neither side wanted me dead.

I took note of how hard the regulators worked as they hissed above me. They could maintain pressure well, assuming we didn't drop too fast.

My ears did something funny. Sted would only risk a drop like that if he thought our lives depended on it.

I, however, couldn't do anything about that. Rick was my priority.

"Hey, Rick, I get that you have your orders, but you know I'm a solid navigator. If we've gotta get outta here, Sted's the man on the controls, but I'm the man to give him direction."

The subtrans lurched again, and I smacked my ear against the bulkhead. It didn't feel good. My head did something funny. I still wasn't back to my normal self.

"Sorry, Teran," Rick replied. "You know when Marda gives orders…."

I laughed. I had Rick now. "Hey, I get it. What Marda says, goes. No one knows that better than me."

He and a few others chuckled as Sted turned sharply again. Rick would trust me now, even though he wouldn't pull the bag. I still couldn't hear any signs of Handler. If they'd brought him, they wouldn't be as kind to him, but I might be able to convince them to keep him alive.

Someone cleared his throat. Gerry. Of course he'd be here. The young man was loyal to a fault, and Rick relied on him for just about everything.

The sound and rhythm of the subtrans changed. We had entered the caves. They were dangerous places if you didn't know your way through. Sted never knew, but he always managed to get out again.

A few minutes later, Sted called out, "I think we lost them."

"Take us home," Rick responded.

I sensed someone sit down beside me. "Hey buddy," Rick began, "what did they do to you?"

I shook my head, hoping it might dislodge the bag somewhat, but no luck. "All I remember is I woke up in a hospital bed. Don't remember anything before that. But…" I paused and lowered my voice to give the impression that I might be struggling with what had happened. "They… I… my arm…"

"What's with your arm?" Rick asked, the concern evident in his voice.

"They said I was in an accident." I paused again and took a deep breath. I let it out slowly, dropping my chin to my chest. "I lost my arm, Rick." I added a choke to my voice. "They replaced it."

There was silence for a while. No one in the subtrans moved. I suspected that meant they all knew and cared for me.

"Let me check."

I felt fingers probe my right forearm, upper arm, shoulder, and chest. I heard a shuffle of feet across the floor of the subtrans, and Rick felt my left arm as well.

"Hey!" I let out an uncomfortable laugh. "Only the one arm."

"Just checking," Rick replied. "We'll need to do a full scan soon."

"Of course." I hoped Handler hadn't authorized the implantation of a tracking device. Such a move was often implemented on suspects, but not on trusted agents. It would be difficult to regain Sigma's trust if I happened to be transmitting our location to UnWoN.

I felt another shift, and our speed picked up significantly. We were out of the caves, likely on our way to Havana.

That meant I had less than five hours to perfect my cover story. I had to include the possibility of a tracking device and perhaps even Handler's presence.

The subtrans slowed down, went through some strange maneuvers, and we connected with something. The door to my right hissed, and a moment later, I heard it slide open.

"We're here, Teran." An arm grasped my elbow. Not roughly. That was a good sign. Rick cleared his throat and added, "Marda's going to want to see you right away."

"Is that a good thing?"

"You're a better judge of that kind of thing than I am, Teran. We just have to be sure."

> *Assess: I need to regain Marda's trust.*
> *Decide: Create the assumption that I am more concerned for their security than they are.*
> *Act: ...*

I came to a stop and turned my head in the direction I knew Rick to be standing. When I spoke, I let the humor slide away and dropped my voice to just above a whisper. "Rick, you gotta scan me for any tracking devices. I…" I shook my head. "I don't know how long I was out or what all they did to me."

He squeezed my arm and matched the volume of his voice to mine. "No worries, buddy. We've got this. You wrote the protocols, remember?"

I did. And I'd been thorough. Unfortunately.

We moved through a series of corridors. Havana's base was right near two exits—one on the north and one on the northeast. From the turns and sounds, I thought we might be at the one on the north.

Ten minutes later, Rick told me to sit. I was grateful. As strong as I felt, I also knew things were still a little off. The bag didn't help.

"Scan him," Rick ordered.

It was generally something you couldn't feel, but I thought for sure I could sense the scan move across my body. Likely just nerves.

Rick spoke again. "Pull it off."

I blinked a few times as my eyes adjusted. Rick nodded to me before he and Gerry walked out of the room.

To my right, the door clicked shut behind the two men. Ahead, a two-way mirror showed my reflection. To my left… Handler.

I wanted to cry out his name. His chest still moved, which gave me some relief, but his face was a mess. I suspected some of it was from the explosion at the hospital, but the rest looked like a few of the members of Sigma had roughed him up.

He opened his one eye just a bit and shook his head. He was right. Best not to say anything in case I said the wrong thing.

I turned back to the door on my right just as it opened. A woman in her mid-thirties—about my age—walked in. She barely glanced at me, which was far more than she did for Handler.

When she reached the center of the room, about three steps in front of me, she stopped without turning to face me. Her eyes remained on the floor, and a tear streamed down her cheek.

Marda had always been an emotional one around me. Far too open. Far too trusting. Far too compassionate. She had been easy to manipulate. From her, I had gained all the intel and access I had sought.

> *Assess: Tears suggest she either missed me or felt betrayed. The lack of eye contact suggests the latter—grief over a sense of betrayal. Her emotions will be difficult to manipulate, but not impossible. She had always hoped there might be more between us than there had been.*
> *Decide: Match her worry.*
> *Act: …*

"Marda," I choked. "What's going on? You guys rescued me. I get that you had to scan me to make sure, but the fact that you're not digging a tracker out of my leg suggests I'm clean. What are you…?" I paused and swallowed before taking a deep breath, letting my voice come out shaky. "Marda, tell me what's going on. What's changed?"

She slowly turned toward me, keeping her eyes on the floor at first. She bit her bottom lip, closed her eyes, and more tears flowed. When she opened them, she met my gaze.

I was wrong. It was not grief in those eyes.

That was hatred.

I gasped, giving just enough of a reaction. "Marda." I let my voice come out small and weak. "Why... you've never looked at me like that... Marda?"

The tears flowed more freely, and I caught sight of a glimmer of hope in her eyes. I had her. Just a little more, and I'd be back in her good books. The one part of my mission I had failed to complete was to kill Marda. I wouldn't fail this time. UnWoN would likely retrieve me within the day. I had that long to finish the job.

"What do you want?" she asked, the familiar authority back in her voice.

I let my face fill with disbelief and confusion. "What do I want?" I shook my head. "What do you mean? I want the same things I've always wanted." I dropped my voice to a whisper again and glanced toward the door, then the two-way mirror. My hands were still bound behind me, but I leaned forward in my chair. "Marda, what's wrong? What's changed? I..." My eyes drifted to my right arm. "It's not my arm, is it? I didn't have a choice. Besides, they said my natural arm was too damaged. Would you rather I not have an arm at all?"

"It's not your arm."

"Then what is it?"

She walked to the side of the room where Handler sat, slumped in his chair. Without any sign of concern for him, she grabbed the back of the chair, and Handler rolled to the floor. I kept my reaction to a minimum. A moment later, she sat across from me on Handler's chair.

"How do I know I can trust you?" she barked. There was hope there, but there was a lot of anger. A lot. There was also something else, but I couldn't put my finger on it.

"It's me, Marda!" I shook my head and closed my eyes. I let my face fill with grief. "I didn't ask for whatever happened to me. I don't even remember it. I just woke up in an UnWoN hospital. They told me it was New Paris and that I had a synthetic arm and kidney. What am I supposed to do about all that?" I paused again. With Marda, it had never been what I said, but pausing at the right time. I could see the hope grow in her eyes as I took a few deep breaths. "Give me a shot of alethon. Strap an old polygraph on me if you want. I don't care!" I hated the feeling of alethon in my system, but I was one of the few people who could lie with it coursing through my veins.

"Neither of those will work on you."

I stared at her for a moment, letting shock fill my face. Truthfully, I *was* shocked. I didn't know how she could know that. "What do you mean, Mar?" I hoped using my little nickname for her might help make the conversation less of an interrogation and remind her of what we once had. "Why won't they work on me?"

She let her eyes drop to the floor again and took a deep breath. Something had changed. I didn't know what, but I'd won another small victory.

She turned her head back to the two-way mirror. A moment later, I heard three sharp taps from the other side. A signal—hopefully good.

"Okay… Teran." She struggled to say my name. She must have been more upset at me than I had thought.

She stood and walked to the door. Without looking back, she stopped and added, "Teran, we're taking a chance. Your access codes are still active. You can… step back into your post. But we're going to need to take you to The Canal."

"Sure," I replied. "I don't know why, but I trust you, Marda. Whatever you need. We're in this together. We always have been."

Her shoulders slumped. Yet another victory. It would not be long before I had regained her trust. I wouldn't kill her until I had a means of escape, but that opportunity would present itself soon enough.

When she opened the door, she ordered, "Untie him," and she was gone.

Rick came in and drew his knife.

"Glad that's over," I said. "Do you know what's got her so spooked?"

Rick didn't reply. He moved around behind me and a moment later, my bonds slid away. I ignored Handler, but out of the corner of my eye, I saw him stand, rubbing his wrists.

"We have to move." Rick pointed toward the door. "After you."

Assess: Rick is far colder toward me than he had been before. Something affected his attitude. It was either the conversation with Marda or the scan.
Decide: The conversation had gone well. The scan…
Act: …

"Was there something in the scan I should be worried about?"

Rick turned his head slightly to me and smiled. "No worries, buddy. There was no tracking device. It really just showed us the extent of their work on you."

That concerned me. "Did they not do a good job?"

He shook his head and laughed. "No worries there either, buddy. They actually did a great job. Doctor Larries checked it over quickly. Their work was top-notch."

"Then what's the problem? Why does Marda want to take me to The Canal?" The Canal housed Sigma's primary medical facilities. They wanted a closer look at something.

Rick stopped and put his hand on my arm. He gripped tightly. "Teran. Just relax, buddy. Trust us. You'd do the same thing if it were one of us. In fact, your protocols call for a lot of this."

I nodded. "You're right, man. Sorry. I think I'm just a little jittery after all that's happened."

He laughed again. "Is the great Teran having a moment of weakness?" He shook his head and chuckled as he started down the hallway. "I thought I'd never see the day."

I glanced back to see Handler following close behind. No other guards. That was a good sign.

Handler shuffled up next to me. He was not a field agent, but he had a gift for assessing the situation. He mouthed the word, "Timing."

I nodded, and he backed off. He was right. I'd need to wait for the perfect moment. Marda would die when I had the opportunity. I had not had the chance to check out what my new arm could do, but I'd heard the high-end synthetic arms could tear a person limb from limb. It would all depend on how much time I had when the moment came.

Halfway to the port, the floor shook just slightly. That was no current. That was an explosion.

"What was that?" I called out, adding a little panic to my voice.

Rick ran to a wallscreen and punched in a code. "Marda! What's going on?"

Marda's voice answered back, "We've been infiltrated. ADAs. Get Teran to the northeast subtrans! Fast!"

Chapter Three

"Let's go, buddy!" Rick called out.

We raced down the hallway with Handler in tow. If ADAs were here, UnWoN didn't expect anyone to survive. Those things were like my new arm. Strong, mechanical, and fast, these creatures received their names from their simple yet direct decision-making process. UnWoN only had a few hundred of them on each continent—too expensive to make more—but they were effective in ending any resistance.

Despite still recovering, I kept up with Rick as we wove our way through the corridors. If we were heading to the northeast subtrans, it was likely a ten minute run. I briefly considered running in the opposite direction to make it to the ADAs—they'd be programmed to protect me—but then any hope of Sigma's continued trust would be gone. I had to play my part until there was no other option.

I heard no sound of fighting at first, but then it came. The familiar sound of Sigma's gunfire, and the unfamiliar sound of ADA projectiles as they zipped through the air. I had learned about them at one time and even studied pictures, but never seen one in action.

I lost my footing and hit the ground hard, Handler landing on top of me. I didn't yet know what had happened, but debris littered the floor. Another explosion. It was a good thing we were still far from the outer hull.

I pulled Handler to his feet and gave him a shove forward. Rick was on his knees, dazed. I grabbed him with my right arm and lifted him right onto his feet. He still seemed shocked, but nodded as we took off down the hallway after Handler.

I turned back to see a gaping hole in the wall nearly thirty feet back the way we'd come. Through the dust and smoke, four sets of red eyes moved forward. ADAs.

ADAs were not only deadly with their strength, speed, and agility, but they were designed to strike fear in the hearts of their victims with their glowing red eyes, humanoid bodies, bare steel teeth, and clawed hands.

I realized just a moment too late that with the dust and smoke, their sensors might not properly identify me. I ran as the zip of the ADA projectiles flew around me. Handler and then Rick disappeared around the next turn, and I had just about made it when one of their darts caught me.

I cried out, but managed to keep running. I reached back as I turned the corner. It had hit me on the right side, lower back.

I ran hard and caught up to Handler and Rick. Somehow, knowing ADAs were on my tail, trying to kill me, gave me the extra speed I needed—despite the dart lodged in my new kidney.

I glanced back, and a jolt of fear shook me. The ADAs were fast—and they didn't seem to worry about gravity. Two of them, using their claws, raced along the ceiling, while the other two moved below them on all fours.

I yanked the dart out of my back. At that point, I needed the maneuverability. I would have to risk internal bleeding and hope we could reach The Canal in time.

Another projectile zipped along and just barely missed my shoulder. They still hadn't identified me yet.

We came upon our last turn, the subtrans port only another dozen feet away, when the first of the ADAs reached us. Once the ADAs identified me, they would fight and make it look real to maintain my cover, but they would not seriously harm me. But Rick would never survive an encounter, and I needed him alive. Until I was definitely finished with Sigma, Rick was my best contact.

I twisted around just as the first one lunged for me. I made sure my face was quite visible. It would only need a fraction of a second to identify me and adjust.

I grabbed it with my right arm and tossed it as hard as I could into the wall behind me, my synthetic arm giving the extra push needed to incapacitate the ADA. The next one slammed into me, knocking me back into the wall.

I pulled my arms free and grabbed its head and twisted, hoping to wrench the thing clean off its neck. Instead, the head just spun all the way around. I grabbed under its chin and ripped upward.

The body of the ADA dropped to the ground. I smiled. I could get used to having a synthetic arm.

The next ADA slammed its fist into my chest, but it didn't hurt. Their programming had kicked in. The robot would understand by now that I was not only their ally, but also that I would need to incapacitate all four of them.

I threw the third ADA into the wall and used the fourth like a bat to smash the third as it recovered. Before either could get back on their feet, I rushed into the subtrans.

The door slid closed, the port hissed, and we lurched forward.

Through the glass porthole, I caught sight of an ADA watching us rush away from Havana.

I turned around, and Rick put the subtrans on auto. I thought that was odd at first, but then saw the urgency in his eyes.

Blood seeped from my belly where another projectile had struck me.

"It looks like it went straight through," Rick said as he calmly tied a bandage around my waist, also covering my wound near my right kidney. "We'll be at The Canal in about twenty minutes. You just have to keep from bleeding out until then."

I laughed. "I'll see what I can do about that."

He returned a smile and then moved back to the pilot's seat and took the subtrans off auto while I examined Handler. He was in decent shape and waved me away. I could see the stress in his eyes. He was holding up well, considering.

I moved to the cockpit and sat next to Rick for a moment or two. I found myself reaching for the console out of habit, but I needed them to learn to trust me. Jumping in now was probably a bad idea. I moved back again with Handler.

Only twenty minutes to The Canal…

If Marda survived the ADA assault and made it to there, then I still needed to finish my mission.

The subtrans lurched, followed by the familiar hiss. A moment later, the door slid open.

Front and center stood Marda. When her eyes landed on me, her expression filled with relief, but then the distrust from earlier returned.

"Bring him, Rick."

I glanced at Handler. He was already getting to his feet. He stepped up next to me and whispered, "We're running out of time. You'll have to take her out soon."

I nodded. He was right. I thought I had won her over, but I had misjudged the situation. The distrust was deep, wherever it came from. I might not be able to keep her on my side.

The pain in my abdomen had lessened. A quick look down revealed the bleeding had stopped.

On the way, I leaned in toward Rick. "Looks like I'm in Marda's bad books again."

He nodded grimly. "Just don't be smart with her right now, Teran. Things are tense. We need to figure out our next steps."

"Of course." I didn't know what we were talking about in terms of steps, but I'd play along. Until my opportunity arose.

I counted the guards along the way. Two or three I could handle. By the time I reached the medical wing of The Canal, I had counted fifty-four. All armed with pulse cannons in their arms and slides on their hips.

The slides concerned me. Rick had one on his hip as well, picked up from Marda after we arrived.

The pulse cannons were pretty common in Sigma. They could hurt, but were designed to knock you down or drive you back. They were also effective against ADAs, but only to slow their advance.

The slides, however, were unusual. A slide delivered a surge of electricity into the target—enough to incapacitate a human and enough to potentially fry the circuits of an ADA.

Either Sigma thought we were about to be attacked by another swarm of ADAs, or they planned on zapping someone. I'd only been hit by a slide surge once. Never wanted to experience that again.

The bigger issue, however, was that every guard had their eye on me. Not on Rick. Not on Handler. On me.

Even my synthetic arm wouldn't get me through all of them.

"In here." Rick opened a door, and Handler and I walked in.

Handler took a seat off to the side. No one seemed to care where he went. Me, on the other hand… I was their focus. The table in the center of the room was obviously reserved for me.

Marda's voice came through a speaker. "Lay down on the table, Teran."

I did as I was told, and Rick strapped me in. I couldn't help but notice that the restraints were reinforced. I thought I might be able to free my right arm, but the rest of me was secured in place until someone released me.

Once he had finished, Rick left the room, shutting the door and locking it behind him. I was not in a good spot.

"Just relax, Teran," Handler whispered to me. "Don't let it get to you. You just have to convince them to trust you again."

I could just barely make out voices in the other room. Only a glass barrier separated them from me, but the curtain was drawn. Three different voices: Marda, a doctor I vaguely remembered, and another woman. I assumed Rick was back there as well.

"The scan... in just a moment..." The doctor's voice was quiet.

"What will it tell us?" Marda asked. Her voice always carried well.

"I don't think we'll know until it's finished," the other woman added, "but we'll know exactly what UnWoN did to him.

"But they'd know we'd be suspicious," Rick added, joining in. "This doesn't make sense."

"Let's just do... and find out... can..." the doctor said.

I closed my eyes. I could figure this out. Something was causing a great deal of suspicion. Something I hadn't yet considered. The arm... no... that couldn't be it. My arm was likely far more sophisticated than anything Sigma had access to, but it was still just an arm.

The kidney… that was it. A second kidney was beneficial, but unnecessary. Many people survived with only one. UnWoN replaced mine—I assumed it was so I could continue to function for them at optimal health— but there was more to the kidney than UnWoN had told me.

I forced down a smile. I knew my employers were up to something. It wouldn't be bad, whatever they'd done. And I didn't mind. I just wish they'd said something. I could be making better use of whatever advantage it gave me.

I heard the scanner start up. It whirred as it moved over me, leaving my skin and insides tingling.

It didn't take long. I heard a gasp or two from the other room, but Marda remained silent.

"Do… see it?" the doctor asked.

"I don't know what I'm looking at," Marda replied. She was getting emotional again.

The doctor's voice came through again, but this time it was louder, and she spoke with more intensity. "There."

"I still don't know what I'm looking at," Marda's frustrated voice came through.

"That's real… that's a problem."

"That's real?" Marda asked. "What does that mean?"

"I don't… but it might mean… Teran…"

"And—" Marda began, but her words choked out at first. "And the other thing?"

The other woman spoke again. "We can deal with that. It's not transmitting, which is good. We don't know what it's for, but I can't imagine it's good."

I turned my head to Handler. His face had gone pale, and he shook his head violently. As he spoke, his voice raised in intensity and volume. "You can't let them take that out, Teran. No matter what, that's the key to all this!" By the time he finished speaking, his voice came out in a shriek.

He was right. Whatever it was, it had to stay.

Assess: I'm strapped to the table, but my right arm could likely break the restraints. If I can free that arm, I might be able to free the rest of me before they come in and use a slide on me.
Decide: Marda would have to die in the next few minutes, or I'd never get another shot at it.
Act: …

I wrenched my arm up against the restraints, and within a second, the straps had ripped free of the table. I pulled at the restraint across my chest, but I couldn't get the leverage at that angle, nor could I reach across to my left arm.

I twisted my body, hoping to reach farther, and the strap across my chest came loose. Rick had been sloppy.

I sat up and even the strap holding my left hand came loose. Maybe Rick was on my side.

"Security!" Marda hollered, "Get in there!"

The door swung open as I tore away the restraints holding my legs. One of the guards shot me with the pulse cannon, and it knocked me back off the table and against the wall.

I recovered quickly and charged, but another shot from a pulse cannon slammed me back again. Before I could move again, Rick stepped into the room, drew his slide, and blasted me with it. The last thing I remembered seeing was Handler's terrified expression as he huddled in the corner, weeping.

Chapter Four

I came to on a table.

A searing pain shot like lightning across my scalp. I cried out, and a group of masked people around the table grabbed my arms and legs.

I struggled, but they were not the only thing holding me in place. Bands held me down, and these were steel. One even ran across my forehead, securing my head and preventing any movement.

"Hold him!" I recognized the doctor's voice, the one who'd spoken with Marda and Rick on the other side of the glass before they used the slide on me. "I've almost got it."

> *Assess: They're trying to incapacitate me.*
> *Decide: Singular priority—escape.*
> *Act: …*

I pulled and thrashed and struggled, attempting to twist my body and gain even a little. No matter how hard I tried, I could not move.

The doctor stood above my head. A sick feeling of horror swept over me. She had my scalp peeled back and my skull cut open. She was doing something to my brain.

I caught sight of Handler through the various masked people. His eyes were filled with terror, and the tears just streamed down his face. I knew I could count on him for strategy and direction, but I was the only one who could get the two of us out of here.

"Got it!" the doctor said.

I screamed.

My voice warped and cracked until I ran out of air, but still I tried to scream some more. My fingers and toes shook.

I looked for Handler but couldn't catch sight of him. The masked people crowded around, shoulder to shoulder.

"Teran!"

I looked to my right, unable to move my head. Marda stood there. I couldn't make sense of her expression behind the mask covering her mouth. Her eyes looked angry, disgusted, worried… maybe even a little relieved.

"Breathe, Teran!"

I tried. I no longer remembered how to take a breath.

Something slipped over my mouth and air passed into my lungs. When they pulled it away, my breathing had resumed.

"Whoa!" That was the woman I had heard from behind the glass. "Look at that."

Marda stepped out of sight, back where they'd worked on my brain.

My mind raced. I felt panicked. I couldn't think straight. I needed Handler, but he was still out of sight.

"Look at it heal," the woman said. "I haven't put any stitches in. It just… healed up. Like the wounds in his abdomen and back."

Marda stepped into view again. "Teran, can you understand me?" This time, without the mask, her expression was clear. Relieved. Definitely relieved. But perhaps also concerned.

I tried to nod but couldn't move my head. "I can."

"Do you know where you are?"

"The Canal."

"Do you know what we've just done?"

"No."

She looked back at the doctor for confirmation, then back at me.

Assess: …
Assess: …
Assess: …

I couldn't think. I had to do something. Kill someone. I didn't know who. I think Marda. Handler would tell me.

The restraint across my forehead released, and I lifted my head for a moment. I felt strong—like I did before they attacked me. I felt ready to move. Ready to fight. Ready to kill.

Someone needed to die. Someone… but…

"Where's Handler?"

Marda's expression changed. "Who?"

"Handler. He was right over there."

Marda looked at me with compassion. "I don't know who this handler is."

"When you rescued me from UnWoN, he was with me. He's been following Rick and me around this entire time. He was just over there against the wall."

The people in masks stepped aside, giving me a clear view. No Handler. I needed him. Now more than ever. Handler had always been there.

I turned my head back to Marda. She looked different. No longer the hard, angry rebel leader. No longer the Sigma dictator. No longer the killer of the innocent. No longer the butcher of the weak and needy. She was familiar. I knew her. I knew her well.

I gasped. "We're... married..."

Her confused expression came back again. "Um... yes, Teran. We are."

I stared at her again for a moment. "You're not the leader of Sigma, are you?"

She shook her head.

It all came back in a rush. I remembered founding Sigma—just Rick and me at first. Then Sted. Then Marda joined. We'd hit it off right away. We were married within a year, even before Sigma was truly on UnWoN's radar.

"What happened to me?"

"Can we release him?" Marda asked the doctor.

A pause. "I... I really don't know, Marda. I have no idea if he's himself... or... who he is."

That confused me, but there was a lot of confusion going around.

"Release him," Marda ordered.

The restraints came off, and Marda helped me sit up. She seemed weak, actually. The truth was, I could tell she did nothing to help me. I felt heavy—too heavy for Marda to lift.

I swung my legs to the side and dropped down. Everyone stepped back just a little. I knew why. I was strong. Not just stronger than average. I was...

I glanced back at the table. The restraints from earlier had been reinforced, but I had snapped them with little trouble. The restraints on this table were bars of steel, some nearly an inch thick. And the one that had held my chest was... bent.

Assess: ...
Assess: ...
Assess: ...

I shook my head to clear my thoughts. "What's happened to me?"

Marda stepped up to me and put her hands on my arms. Rick, standing by the door, tried to be discreet, but I noticed his hand move toward his slide. Beside him, Gerry stood, also with his hand on his slide.

"UnWoN took you," Marda said, her voice choked as she spoke. "About a month ago. It took us that long to find you. We thought you were in Moscow, then in Berut, then in... well... it doesn't matter. We found you. But, when Rick and Sted got you out, you were... different."

I stretched my neck a bit, along with my shoulders. I certainly was different. Something was off. I was… better than before.

More memories flooded back. "The scans… what did they show?"

Marda's eyes filled with tears, and her lips trembled. She opened her mouth to speak, but nothing came out. She nodded to someone.

A woman stepped up beside Marda. I remembered her. A doctor—a neurologist maybe… or maybe just a GP… everything was still fuzzy.

"I'm Doctor Swent, if you don't remember. UnWoN did some serious work on you."

"My arm, shoulder, and kidney. Yes, I know."

She shook her head. "No, Teran. They replaced more than that."

I frowned at her. "How much?"

She glanced at Marda, who appeared ready to break into tears.

The doctor turned back to me and closed her eyes for a moment. When she opened them, she gave me a look of genuine compassion. "Teran, the only thing that is still you… still the old Teran… is your brain. Everything else was replaced."

I stumbled back against the table. I began to shake my head violently back and forth and raised my fist at the doctor.

A man beside me lunged forward and grabbed my arm, but I pushed him away.

I stared in shock at the man as he crumbled to the floor, a good ten feet from me.

The doctor rushed to his side, checked his pulse. "He's alive. Get him onto the table." She turned to Marda. "I'm sorry, Marda, but you've got to get Teran out of the operating room. I need to help this man."

Marda pulled me along and out the door. Rick followed close behind. He'd drawn his slide, but I was glad he hadn't used it.

"How did I do that?" I asked quietly. "I just pushed him. He was a big guy. Like… well over two hundred pounds. His feet left the ground… I threw him… how?"

Marda put her hands on my arms again. I remembered. She did that a lot when she needed me to focus. I concentrated on her.

Her voice choked again as she explained. "We don't understand it all, but they seem to have transplanted your brain into an ADA's body. We weren't really even sure it was you for a while. We… discovered a tiny chip implanted in your brain. Doctor Swent removed it."

My mind spun, but one question held on. "You still haven't told me where Handler went."

She shook her head. "I don't know who this handler is."

"He's been with me the entire time. He's been with me for most of my life, actually. I remember him with me even as a child."

"Did he disappear when we removed the chip?" she asked.

"I…" The memories of Handler all through my life were fading. I thought he had always been there, but none of the memories made sense. What I could remember was now distant. In all my life, he never aged.

Never changed. Even his clothes… always the same outfit.

It all came clear. My voice came out in just above a whisper. "Handler was the chip." Panic filled my chest… or my mind. I didn't know what was me. "Am I even human anymore?"

Marda's eyes dropped, and the tears streamed down her face. "I don't know, Teran. I don't know anything. I don't know what to think or how to feel. Doctor Swent thought it was still you, but she's just guessing. We really don't know. If it is you in there…" she swallowed hard. I could see her struggle to maintain control. In a whisper, she said, "If it's still you, I still want you."

I felt… grateful. Relieved. And horrified that she would have to love an ADA.

"Wait." A memory from earlier in the day came rushing back, and I closed my eyes to try to see it clearly. "When I was in the subtrans… with Rick… I…" I tried to focus on the memory. It was difficult to hold on to it, but I knew one thing. "UnWoN… they know we were headed here to The Canal." I opened my eyes. "They'll be here soon."

Rick shook his head. "How do they…"

An explosion rocked the base. Most people higher up in the city would not even feel the shudder, but whatever had happened was close.

"Report!" I hollered, stepping back into my role.

Gerry hesitated for a moment before checking his pad. "There seems to have been an explosion at the main port." His face turned white, and his mouth dropped open.

"Give me the information I need, soldier!" In a moment of threat, I needed answers.

"Sorry, sir," Gerry said as he pulled himself together. "The entire east end of the base is flooded. East is not an option."

Another explosion, but this one farther away. The man checked his pad. "That's the north port."

"We go up!" I declared. I didn't know if Sigma expected me to take command again. They might not trust me. Truthfully, I didn't trust myself, but there was no time for indecision. I turned to Marda. "Get everyone into the city. We'll meet at Taco's."

Marda hesitated. "But that's the least secure safe house we have!"

I nodded. "Make it happen. I'll explain on the way."

She paused for just a moment longer before passing out orders. Rick immediately went into action. Marda's strength lay in coordinating the many divisions of Sigma, while Rick was the one to make it all happen.

I pointed at two guards, plus Rick and Marda. "You four with me."

We ran down the corridor and turned right, then right again. In a few minutes, we were at a hatch leading up. We pulled a small ladder out, and I spun open the hatch. One of the men with us whistled as I did so. Those hatches were notoriously difficult to turn. I tried not to think too much about why I had that kind of strength.

Once we were all through the hatch, I reached down, grabbed the ladder from above, and did my best to toss it back to the wall. I didn't want to leave any indication we'd gone this way, but I also didn't want to remove the ladder in case other members of Sigma needed to use this exit.

I sealed the hatch, and we raced down a hallway littered with trash and the occasional sleeping man or woman. The lower levels of each city always contained the greatest signs of UnWoN's effect on the world. Their control of every aspect of people's lives and thoughts and beliefs had initially left anyone who did not agree to fend for themselves. In recent years, UnWoN had decided that removal of all dissenters was their only option.

It was the bloodbath that came as a result of their purge that birthed Sigma, along with dozens of other rebellions. Now, years later, Sigma remained as the only surviving resistance.

We covered our faces just before we stepped out among the crowds and entered a street filled with those deemed unacceptable by UnWoN. People here walked cautiously, careful to avoid moving in any manner that might attract attention. Cameras sat on every corner, identifying anyone without a hood and keeping a record for future punishment of all those who stepped out of line.

"Slow down!" a guard bellowed.

Chapter Five

We slowed, but dared not raise our heads enough to acknowledge the guard. It would only take a second, and my image would be sent to UnWoN's computers. We'd be surrounded in minutes.

I glanced back at Rick. He'd hidden his slide well under his jacket. I assumed his pulse cannon had already been discarded. We had instituted that policy years before. Pulse cannons were far too bulky for travel in the city.

The farther down the street we moved, the thicker the smell. The recyclers rarely worked well at these levels. At least the pressure regulators functioned properly. Moscow had once had an uprising in the lower sections of the city. UnWoN had turned off the regulators for only a minute, and no one below Level Eighty survived.

"Up here!" I hissed, and we ran up a flight of stairs leading from Level One-Eighty-Two, the lowest official level in The Canal, up to One-Eighty-One, then one more again. When we reached the street, we slowed down enough to avoid notice and moved toward the elevators. Once there, we paid our fare along with another sixty or so people, and a moment later, we were on our way up.

I did my best to look around at the faces on the elevator without revealing mine. I couldn't identify too many, but I caught glimpses of a few people I recognized. Doctor Swent had made it out. She rarely left the lower base in the city. She stood with her head down, doing her best not to stand out, along with a few others. I was pleased to see the man I had injured back on his feet and standing beside her, despite his need for her support.

When we reached Level One-Fifty, we stepped off into a street not much different from the litter-filled, poverty-stricken lower sections, although this area was packed with people. One-Fifty was a transfer level. Elevators moved from here to various levels and a train system took passengers to the other side of the city.

The other difference in this area had to do with speed. Since so many transferred to the elevators or trains on their way to work, people often ran. UnWoN soldiers rarely took notice.

We raced off down the street, taking an indirect route to avoid running alongside too many members of Sigma.

When we reached the trains, we loaded on, careful to find a car with no soldiers. We found seats at the rear of the car and kept our voices low.

"Why Taco's?" Marda asked before I could bring it up.

"I know it's an obvious choice," I explained, "but one of many. It's also near the generators. Sometimes transmissions can't move through that area well. I expect we'll meet an ADA or two. Due to the interference, they won't be able to call for help, and we can move on from there to our next target."

Rick leaned in. "Target? I thought we were on the run, not on mission."

I turned to Rick and glared at him. He backed off, and I noticed his hand moved just slightly toward the slide, which I could just barely make out inside his jacket. "Look at what they've done, Rick! They've managed to infiltrate us by turning me into a monster. They'll go to any length! Do you know what I was planning on doing just before you shot me with the slide?"

He shook his head.

I turned to Marda. "I had orders to kill. The ADA chip inside my brain didn't just give me visions of Handler; my marching orders were to kill you!"

She took in a sharp breath. "Why me?"

"Think about it." I felt the rage build inside. I didn't know if I was still human, but I did feel anger. "If the leader of Sigma steps in and kills not only his second in command, but also his wife, the woman he loves, everything falls apart. We're the only ones left standing against UnWoN." I took a deep breath and wondered if I even needed to breathe anymore or if it was just an unnecessary process. "If we turn on each other— especially the two of us—then Sigma is finished. And so is any chance of bringing UnWoN's control to an end." I shook my head. I think I would have normally cried right now, but the tears didn't come. Perhaps they never would again. "Marda, I would have killed you without a moment's remorse." I clenched my fists. "They did this to us!"

I turned back to Rick. "We are *not* on the run. We are on mission! We will continue to be on mission until we put an end to UnWoN. They have made hiding impossible. We can't strike from the shadows anymore. It's time we take the fight to them."

The train shuddered, and I felt the change in movement. The lights shifted as we entered the station.

"This is it," Rick said.

We made our way to the doors along with dozens of others. Mechanics and divers and pressure technicians and structural repair techs. Farmers and shopkeepers and service workers. The general population moved without passion, without hope. That would all change soon. UnWoN would be held to account.

Half-way out of the station, I caught sight of Doctor Swent and Gerry. I made eye contact briefly with Gerry, but we both looked away. UnWoN's computers analyzed where people looked and who appeared to know one another. Guilty by association remained a continual threat, looming over every public interaction.

At first, we moved east down the street, then to the north, then to the east again, doing our best to zigzag through the area. Taco's was just ahead.

We reached the doors of the abandoned restaurant and walked right on by. After circling around back, we climbed in through a window. Occasionally, we found homeless men and women living inside, but this time, it lay empty. Only the remains of a few blankets and empty cans of rations. From the looks of things, the former occupants had not left willingly.

We settled in out of sight of the uncovered windows in the front of the old store. Smashed computers and stoves littered the old ceramic tiles. The place had been in use when I was a kid. I remembered punching in my order and watching the stoves fire up to produce a taco in just under ten seconds. The place had been one of the most popular restaurants in the lower levels. It could seat hundreds with standing room for hundreds more.

That was before UnWoN accused the Central American leadership of corruption, removed them, and stepped in to show how much better they were.

No one below Level Fifty thought they were better off. Even the soldiers regretted the change, but they, like the rest of us, had no choice but to follow orders—at least in public.

More members of Sigma trickled in. One of the great things about Taco's was the large windows. From outside, they gave a clear view of much of the inside of the store. Any soldiers passing by would just peek through for a moment on their patrols. For us, there were enough hiding spots that, though the store would appear empty from the front, it was anything but on the inside.

After a while, Marda whispered, "Most of us are here."

I did a quick scan. I estimated over a hundred spread out through the store. Perhaps all that was left of our Canal Base.

I was just about to address the crowd when someone called out a warning. "Something's happening in the street!"

I peered around an overturned table. At first, I could only see people moving quickly along—in a panicked run. But then I caught sight of someone. Through the dirty windows, I couldn't be sure, but it looked like Rick's assistant, Gerry.

"Why's he got his hood down?" Rick whispered. "He'll be recognized!"

A moment later, I knew why.

At least a dozen humanoid steel bodies, glowing red eyes and wicked sharp teeth, stepped into view, moving with inhuman precision.

ADAs.

"Out the back!" I hissed, but the first man through the window cried out, and the next one pulled himself back in.

Marda took in quick reports, then turned to me. "We're surrounded!"

I jumped up and spun around at the sound of the windows at the front of Taco's shattering. "Defensive positions!"

We moved around, distributing the slides we had in our possession, leaving a guard on every exit and every window with at least one. A scream at the back of the restaurant drew my attention. Two ADAs moved like lightning into the crowd, dodging shots from the slides and taking out a half-dozen members of Sigma before my soldiers could land even one clean shot.

From the front of Taco's, Gerry called out, "Surrender, Sigma. It's over."

Before I could answer him, one of the ADAs standing next to Gerry shot him in the head. His lifeless body hit the ground and sent a clear message. There was no surrender. There was no joining with UnWoN.

We were meant to die.

"Hold the line!" I called to Rick.

And then I charged.

Attacking them would not convince them that I was the enemy. Their programming would leave them to assume I was merely protecting my cover. They would only feign their retaliation.

As long as they couldn't confirm my chip was gone…

I reached the first ADA, and it made a feeble attempt to fight back. I pulled its head from its body, and then smashed my fist through the skull of the second, destroying its processing unit.

Before I could reach the third, however, I felt the tingle of a scan moving across my body. It rested on my head for just a moment before the eyes of every ADA in the room turned on me.

It had only taken seconds, but I was now the primary threat.

They zeroed in on me and charged. I grabbed the first ADA by the legs before it could attack and used it like a club. I still had trouble believing the strength in my new body, but I focused on the more important matter—survival.

After smashing four more ADAs, the one in my hands managed to swing its body around and attack. It pulled itself around my shoulders and onto my back, raking my face with its claws.

I screamed and grabbed one of its arms, twisting until the entire ADA came loose and dropped to the floor. I pulled the arm off and drove it fist first through the robot's chest.

Two of the ADAs went down from slide shots. Another ADA moved toward me and had nearly reached me when its body lurched off to the side and smashed against a wall. One of our members must have kept a cannon.

I caught sight of a flash of movement to my left, but before I could react, my body slammed to the ground. At a glance, I counted six ADAs above me. They ripped open my shirt. Four held me down while the other two tore into my chest.

I tried to resist, but their grip was too much. I raised my head while they worked. The pain was excruciating, yet at the same time it felt almost… intellectual, as if I had knowledge of the pain, rather than feeling.

I felt different. I thought different. The blood I saw in my chest sat along the surface of the flesh, but the insides were mechanical, controlled by dozens of tiny computer modules.

I knew what they were after. My power cell. I wrenched my body around to try to twist out from under their weight, but I couldn't budge.

I saw it the same moment they did. It was small—it fit neatly in one of their hands as they pulled it up and slid it out of place.

I made one more attempt to…

Chapter Six

It took me a while to understand.

I could not feel. I could not see. I could not hear. There was nothing. But not the nothing of quiet. There was simply nothing.

With no stimuli, I could only think.

The world that had been no longer felt real to me. All had been a dream. All had been a creation of a silly mind.

I remembered my childhood, my parents, my older sisters, my younger brother. I remembered my friends. I remembered my wife. I remembered marrying her.

It all felt like it could never have existed in this nothingness.

I forced myself to concentrate. To understand.

If my brain had been the only thing still human, it might survive for seconds or even a minute or two without the power cell. It was even possible that the brain's support systems had their own power cell—enough to keep my one human part alive.

That thought encouraged me at first, then made me wonder if I could ever die. Would I live on for centuries, long after those I loved were long gone?

My chest hurt.

That was odd.

My face tingled—although just a little. Somehow, I knew it was healing.

The chest healed as well, but slower. It had further to go.

An irritating screech pulled me from my curiosity. I tried to twist my body to get away from it, but nothing responded. The sound grew louder, then cleared. My hearing had reset.

"…heavier than he looks."

Rick often complained, but never truly minded. He thought complaints were funny.

"You've got the light end. Try carrying his upper body."

Sted. He was young and strong, but I didn't think he'd be able to carry my entire ADA torso, arms, and head.

"Yeah, but you have two guys to my one."

Rick had a point.

"Just keep moving!"

Marda. She always had a plan. Always had a purpose.

The pain in my chest increased. I tried to cry out, but my mouth wasn't back up and running yet. I feared I was more computer now than human. I would need time to reboot.

"Look at his chest."

Another voice. I didn't recognize that one.

"It's like it's… healing."

"He's an ADA," Rick said amidst grunts. "Or at least his body is. I suspect the shell they put around his brain is designed to repair itself."

I took offense at references to me like I was a machine, but set it aside. It was now who I was. It was my future. I *was* a machine.

Any question of purpose was now gone. I had one purpose. End UnWoN. Perhaps now I finally had the tools to accomplish my goal. And it had only cost me my life.

Code flashed before my eyes, followed by images and colors. My optical sensors—my eyes, for lack of a better term—had reset.

I saw Rick, Sted, and a guy named Phillip, I think, above me, carrying my limp body. I didn't see Marda, but I heard her give orders to someone. We were on the run.

Marda stepped into view and announced. "We'll reach Header's Wing in just under an hour."

Header's Wing. Considering the speed they were walking, we'd been traveling for a few hours already. It wouldn't be that long of a trip if we could use the public elevators and trains, but carrying a flesh-covered ADA with a ripped open chest was not something typically done in public. They would have had to use the less visible routes.

"Hey!" someone called out. The tone of voice carried with it a challenge. In these unpatrolled passages, there were often thieves, scoundrels, and even gangs.

A pulse cannon fired, and I heard a group of people scramble to get away. I would have smiled at the thought of Marda refusing to even engage in conversation or negotiation with them if I had control of my lips.

I felt sensation in my fingers and toes. I wiggled them briefly but didn't continue. If I couldn't walk, all my wiggling toes would accomplish would be to distract them.

Any thought of not distracting them disappeared, however, when my vocal processors reset. I felt my mouth open and just about every tone and sound across all human hearing came out of my mouth in a matter of four seconds.

The men dropped me, and Rick drew his slide. Before he could shoot, I called out, "Wait!" I took a few breaths, unsure again if my breaths actually accomplished anything. "It's just me. I'm resetting or… whatever my body does now."

Marda came in close. Tears streamed down her cheeks, and she held my face.

At that moment, I realized I was the luckiest guy in the world. Even with whatever I'd become, my wife still loved me.

Her words came in choking sobs. "I thought we'd lost you. We got your power cell from the ADA, and Rick put it back in. We had no idea if it would work until we saw your chest begin to close up and knit together."

I nodded and smiled, pleased that my lips and neck responded. My body was back under my control.

"I seem to still be alive." I chuckled and pulled myself to my feet, feeling strong and well balanced. A quick glance down at my chest showed unbroken skin. I just needed a new shirt. One that wasn't ripped to shreds and covered in fake blood.

We gathered in a small, abandoned apartment, deep in Header's Wing.

I sat on the floor just under the open window. Marda sat next to me, Rick in the center of the room, and a smattering of others, including Sted, sat around here and there. The Sigma Council had been much larger just a few days before.

However, eight was six more than I had started with ten years ago.

Less than an hour before, UnWoN had announced the capture and death of every Sigma member—despite our own opinions to the contrary. The masses took to the streets immediately and now a riot was fully underway.

I hadn't realized how much the general populace had been counting on us to end the tyranny, the limits, the starvation, the control. To end the reign of those who claimed to be doing all for the good of the people.

"Will it be enough?" Sted asked. "I mean… will they keep going… do you think?"

I shook my head. "No."

Everyone's heads turned to me. I didn't know if I had a soul anymore, but I still knew what people were like.

"The military will stand. They won't use deadly force. But they'll use pulse cannons and drive the people back."

Rick frowned. "Should we be down there?"

I shook my head.

Sted growled. "Then it's been for nothing."

I held Sted's gaze. "No, it hasn't."

I smiled. For the first time since I'd awoken in UnWoN's hospital, I concentrated on what it felt like to smile. It didn't have the same effect on me. It didn't make me feel better. It didn't feel good. But it did feel right.

"We have learned two things." I made eye contact with each of the seven others. "The first thing we've learned is that the people are not only afraid, but they're ready to revolt. The second thing we've learned is the military is standing strong."

"How does that help us?" Rick asked with disgust. "The soldiers will swallow anything they're told by UnWoN."

My smile grew. "No, Rick. They are us!"

His face filled with confusion. He glanced at Marda as if to ask, "Is Teran really all right?"

I raised my hands and laughed. "I'm not still under UnWoN's control, if that's what you're wondering, Rick. We have a problem. The people are almost uniformly against UnWoN. They cry out for freedom, then run and hide. Unfortunately, the military serves UnWoN without question. The military, however, is pulled from the general population."

I stood and waved everyone over to the window. Below, in the streets, the people pushed forward, but a large contingent of soldiers guarding the elevators stood in a row with pulse canons, firing into the crowd. The elevators were the only way to reach UnWoN Control—aside from subtrans. The orders from UnWoN to their soldiers would likely be to hold that spot, no matter the cost.

"Look at the soldiers. Look how they stand, confident and determined. Yet, they've all been conscripted from among us—albeit at a young age. Many of them walk among us, but few ever speak with anyone—except to challenge someone who steps out of line. I have long suspected they are under orders not to speak with us 'common folk'. I don't think they have any idea of what the average person goes through to survive."

Rick leaned a little closer to get a better view. "How does that help us?"

I turned and grabbed his shoulder, careful not to squeeze too hard with my new strength. "We are the ones to tell them—tell the soldiers what they should already know! It's time they understand that they are the ones who are keeping our enemies in power."

I waved everyone to their seats. "I remembered something in Havana, but didn't understand the memory fully until a few minutes ago. I'm the one who informed UnWoN that we were heading to The Canal."

Rick frowned. "How did you do that?"

"I was quick. I did it when I sat down beside you at the console of the subtrans."

He shook his head. "I watched you closely. You did nothing of the sort."

I raised my hand. It was hard to see in the apartment, but each of my friends gasped. Out of the ends of my fingers snaked dozens of tiny wires. "I didn't even think about it at the time, but I tapped into the subtrans' com and sent a message. It took less than a second." I lowered my hand. "They did this to me. But now, all I need is access to UnWoN's system, and a message to deliver. I now have the means to tap into their computers. I can ensure that every soldier receives the message instantly."

Everyone stared at me in shock.

I felt sick to my stomach. The reality of my lack of humanity crashed down hard. They could see it too. I was a monster.

"I know what you think when you look at me," I announced to everyone.

"You can read our minds, too?" Sted asked, raising his hands up as if to ward off my powers.

"No." I took a deep breath. "I know what you're thinking, because I'm thinking it myself. I'm not human anymore. I'm not what I once was. I might be an ADA. I might be a monster. But to take down UnWoN, we need a weapon. I'm that weapon. And they made the mistake of giving it to us."

I let that sink in for a moment, then started handing out orders. "Marda, you're responsible for coming up with the message for the soldiers. Rick, you find me a console that I can access. Sted, you take a couple people and scout out the area."

"What are you going to do?" Marda asked.

"I don't know. I need to figure out what I am."

They rose and set out to fulfill their orders, pulling in others to help as needed. I found a small side room and had a seat on the floor. I closed my eyes and concentrated on my new body. The strength I knew about. The speed the strength afforded would be handy. The ability to access a computer was a useful tool, but something else bothered me.

Now that the chip was gone, I could see my orders a little more clearly. I had thought I was merely to kill Marda, but they didn't want a simple murder.

If I had murdered Marda, it would have left everyone disillusioned and hoping for someone else to come to their aid. But if I had killed Marda in the way UnWoN had wanted, it would have left the people terrified.

I had been ordered to drag her out into public view, place my hands around her throat…

The thought sickened me, but I pushed through. My hands were to…

I opened my eyes and looked down. My fingers and hands looked exactly the way I remembered them. There was even the mole that had been on the back of my left hand since I was a teenager.

But something else…

The room lit up, sparks flying everywhere, as electricity coursed through my hands and arced from finger to finger.

I was to electrocute her. It had been intended to be such a display that no one would see me as anything but a monster. It would utterly destroy their faith in me and in Sigma and in any future rebellion.

The people's hero was a monster.

I smiled.

It was time for UnWoN to meet their creation.

Chapter Seven

"All right," Marda explained. "The message is contained in this chip. Not only does the information include all the statistics for deaths, starvation, abuse, and more, but it will show video of the ADAs' attack in our Havana base. I've also recorded a bit of personal experience of our suffering and the general populace. I doubt it'll take long before it's seen by the majority of soldiers across the world." She tossed me the chip.

Everyone watched what I would do with it. I suspected they thought I would eat it or something. I put it in my pocket, and I could almost feel their disappointment.

I thanked Marda, and Rick stepped forward. "I tracked one down—a console—but you're not going to like it. The closest UnWoN console, at least one that'll do what you want, is on the fourth floor."

My mouth dropped open. That close to the surface, UnWoN had more security, more soldiers, and more ADAs than I could face.

"Thanks, Rick. Sted?"

"The riots have quieted down a bit, but are still far from calm. They're at a bit of a standoff. We won't get through the elevator. I think subtrans is the way to go."

Marda frowned and put her hand up. Everyone in the room grew silent. "I want to speak with Teran alone."

We didn't have many members of Sigma left, but those we did moved into the dilapidated kitchen. Marda stepped over to the window and stared down into the streets.

"You're up to something, Teran." She spoke softly, but I could hear the fear in her voice. When she spoke again, she was on the verge of tears. "They may have done terrible things to you, but I still know you. What are you up to?"

"You know what I'm up to, Marda." I closed my eyes for a moment before opening them and turning her to face me. "You know it's the only way."

"There's strength in numbers."

I shook my head. "Not this time. The numbers will only lead to more bloodshed."

The tears streamed down her face. "I can't lose you again."

"Then I'd better not fail."

She came in and embraced me. I wrapped my arms around her, although I felt distant. I wasn't the man she married. I never would be again.

When the others came back in, she announced, "Teran is going to the fourth floor alone."

The others grumbled, and Rick growled. "No way, Teran. We're going together!"

"We're not, Rick. I'm the only one who has a chance. If this is going to work, I have to go alone. The rest of you will slow me down, or worse, you'll die."

No one was happy, but they knew I was right. And it was time to move.

"Here's the plan. Your job is to mobilize the people. Get everyone you can to every elevator throughout the city. They should not attack the soldiers, just keep the pressure on. I'll take a subtrans to the fourth floor and finish the job. Remember, the people need to keep the pressure on to distract UnWoN, but the soldiers need to be free enough to receive the intel I'll be sending them— so don't let another riot break out. Keep the balance!"

The men and women in the room nodded.

I stepped forward in line. Dozens of people gathered in the transfer port, looking to get on a subtrans. There were rarely so many from the upper levels this far down in the city, but today seemed to be an exception.

"ID?" the man behind the counter asked.

I handed him one of our recent creations. I didn't think it would hold up to scrutiny on its own, but it didn't need to. As I pulled my hand back, the tiny wires snaked out, connected with his console for just a moment. It didn't take long.

"Ah, Mr. French, I apologize for the wait."

"No worries," I explained, keeping my face down just enough that I hoped the cameras wouldn't identify me. "Is my subtrans ready?"

"Yes, sir," the young man answered. "Will you be needing a pilot today?"

"No, I will be traveling on my own."

The man shifted in his seat. "I recognize this is an unusual request, sir, but as you know, many are trying to get themselves out of the lower levels due to the unpleasantness happening in the streets. The subtrans you have reserved for yourself seats a dozen. We only have two left and over thirty people waiting to travel home. Are you willing to take some of the others with you?"

I leaned in close. This was no time for compassion. I had to appear as an elite. "Does anything about what you see on my ID suggest that I care about these thirty people?"

The man's face drained of color. He shook his head and handed my ID back to me. "Right that way, sir. Your subtrans is number forty-two."

I moved past the people, keeping my hood in place. It would be unusual for a man to walk through this area with his face covered, but no one would question me. The people on the upper levels were often eccentric.

I reached number forty-two and sealed the door behind me. I had heard some grumbling that I was taking one of the last two subtrans, but no one dared challenge a man who could command such privilege.

A few minutes later, the subtrans creaked and the pressure regulators kicked in at full power. I was curious what I could handle. Typically, if I moved up too fast, my ears would pop, and I'd get lightheaded. Nothing of the sort happened this time. I overrode the safety measures and climbed faster. Still no problem.

One more piece of evidence that my humanity was almost entirely gone.

An hour later, I reached the fourth floor and nestled into a port. When my door opened, the inner lock was still sealed, but a quick swipe of my card with a quick hack of the computer and the inner lock clicked and slid open for me.

On the other side, stood three ADAs.

The first two ADAs lunged, and I hit the floor of the subtrans, cracking my head on the steel grating.

Pain shot up through my skull, but I knew it was only a programmed response. My vision remained clear. My actual brain was fine—well protected.

I twisted my body, and the first ADA rolled over the second one. Before the second could react, I swung my leg around and kicked it in the face.

I rolled to the side as the third ADA came at me and shot my arm out, grabbing it as it flew by, spinning it around and twisting its head clean off. I threw the skull at one of the remaining ADAs as it jumped to its feet, and then attacked the other, driving my fist through its chest, grabbing what I thought might be the power supply, and ripping it out.

The ADA dropped to the ground.

The only one remaining took its place in the doorway. I knew it was calling for reinforcements. Somehow, UnWoN had figured out I was coming, but assumed three ADAs would be enough.

In a way, I felt proud—proud that three of their best was not enough. But the reality of the situation crashed down on me. They would not come so unprepared next time.

I glanced down. Sure enough, it was a power supply in my hand. I charge forward, twisting the top off my new weapon, exposing the terminals. When I reached the final ADA, I slammed the power supply into the side of its head, forcing ten thousand volts through the creature's hardware.

I raced out of the subtrans. My only hope was that UnWoN didn't know my purpose. Perhaps they thought I was merely trying to plant a bomb. If that were true, I would likely head to Havana HQ, one floor up.

I ran down a hallway, turning left, then left again, then right, doing my best to move away from the elevator and from any access ports leading up. I circled around, trying to make my way to the console Rick had identified. When I reached my destination, two men stood guard.

The door itself was not much to look at. It was merely a relay station, but it would do.

"What's your business here?" the one man called out as I approached.

I made a show of pulling out my ID as I moved closer. Neither man asked anything else. If I turned out to be someone of consequence, they would not question me further.

I passed on my ID, but before the man could swipe it through his pad, I knocked him back against the wall with such force that he crumpled to the ground. I turned to the other man, watching the expression on his face change. Everything moved so slowly and at first, I thought something was wrong until I understood. I was moving at the same speed as an ADA. I doubted the man could focus on me. I might not be much more than a blur to him.

I slammed my open hand into his chest, careful to knock him out but not cause serious injury. He dropped, and I crouched next to him. A quick search resulted in his security card, and a moment later, I had the door open.

Inside, I found a small room with steel walls and a solid door on the far side. On my left was the only thing of interest in the room—the console.

Before I could move, my body lurched forward, and I slammed up against the wall. Spinning around, I drove my fist through the face of another ADA, and ducked out of the way of the next attack. Back out in the hallway, a dozen or more charged forward.

I let my system speed up enough that the ADAs appeared to have slowed down, finding out that UnWoN had not just made me an ADA, but they had made me better. I ran up the side of the wall, flipping over the next ADA in line, grabbing it by the shoulders, and throwing it out the doorway, knocking the next four down. I dropped my hand onto the computer console, and the thin wires snaked out.

Contact.

Command: Secure a channel to every soldier, on or off duty.

The next ADA was upon me, and I severed the connection. I threw him up against the wall as three others jumped, slamming me to the ground. I could feel them try to rip open my chest. They were going for the power supply.

I brought my knees up and swung my right fist around, dislodging two out of the three ADAs. The third one went for my face, but I grabbed its arm.

Every move I made was faster than anything the ADAs could do, but there were just too many.

I threw the ADA across my chest and jumped to my feet, grabbing the next ADA and using its body to slam the door closed. The lock automatically clicked shut, and I focused on the five ADAs currently in the room. Three were already damaged, but the other two charged.

I ducked and rolled, coming up behind the one, twisting its head off. I rushed the other one, crushing its chest with my shoulder.

The other three injured ADAs tried to overpower me, but they were easily dispatched.

I put my hand on the console, connecting once again with the system.

Command: Transmit message to entire military, individual comms.

The door bulged inwards as the ADAs slammed into it. I only had seconds at most.

Command: Access chip.

A small slot opened, and I pushed the chip inside. The console screen displayed,

Message downloaded.

The door took another hit and two of the three hinges popped. One more hit, and they would be inside.

Command: Send to all.

The door flew inward. I jumped out of the way, narrowly avoiding taking the steel door to my face.

When I got to my feet again, the ADAs didn't come for me. They moved toward the console.

I dove for the closest one, knocking it out of the way. I hadn't thought that they might send a counter message. If it came from the same console, UnWoN could claim it was all a practical joke.

I threw the ADA out of the room and plowed into the others. I had to keep them away. If I destroyed the console, the message might be cancelled.

I ducked and slammed my fist into the chest of another ADA.

There had to be another way.

I took a blow to the face but then knocked the ADA back.

To my left was a porthole.

I grabbed the next ADA and threw it up against the ceiling, kicking it like a football as it dropped to the ground.

I could see a bit of light through the ocean waters. This close to the surface, the sunlight reached the upper levels.

If the area flooded, power would automatically cut, but the message would not be canceled.

An ADA grabbed my shoulder, and I shook it off.

I dove for the side wall and drove my fist through the porthole. Water rushed in. Cold seawater filled my mouth and ears, knocking me back as the airlocks sealed and the power went out.

Chapter Eight

Marda pushed forward with the others. They had managed to get another three or four thousand civilians to move against the soldiers at the elevators.

It was a stand-off. No one moved on either side—for the most part.

Now and then, a man or woman would break out of the crowd and charge the soldiers, but a quick shot from a pulse cannon put an end to it.

"Move another hundred over to that side," Marda ordered. She hoped the movement would keep the tension up. Turning to Rick, she asked, "Any word?"

"We're getting something now…"

She stepped over to him. Rick had hacked into the basic comms for UnWoN. The channel was not secure, but she expected her message would come across that band in addition to most other military controlled comms.

A video of the poverty throughout many of the cities flashed onto the screen, followed by the brutality of the ADAs, hunting down dissidents. The massacres, the cruelty, the executions… people living in fear was evident in just about every shot. Video after video, image after image, popped up on the screen.

Marda watched the soldiers. Most stood staring at the messages coming through on their armbands. They looked confused and unsure.

She sent out orders to the people to back off, allowing the soldiers all the time they needed.

When the video finished, the soldiers stood in shock. Few would ever have seen any of that before. Most of what they were exposed to was colored by UnWoN's unique perspective.

Marda was about to step forward and call for the soldier in charge, but Rick stopped her. "They're doing damage control."

A video popped up showing a group of people led away by soldiers, the report claiming they were hackers who disseminated the false information.

"If they can twist it so quickly, was there any point?" Rick asked.

Marda laughed. "This is the first time the military has been exposed to anything other than what UnWoN has wanted to tell them. Even when they acted against civilians, they were always told the people were the enemy. This is a big win. They've at least heard another side. We now have the opportunity for real change."

Marda examined the soldiers. Men and women shifted on their feet. No one looked confident. Even the officer in charge appeared angry, although not with the rioters.

The seeds of freedom had been planted. They only needed to wait for it to grow.

"There's more!"

She looked down at Rick's comm. The report continued. Not only were most of the supposed hackers immediately arrested, according to the report, but those who had escaped capture had flooded the fourth floor.

Marda's heart went cold, and she put her hand over her mouth. The news was always full of lies, but there was also a note of truth in each report. It would be difficult to fake a huge section of the city flooded.

"Teran," she whispered. "Could he have survived?"

Rick looked unsure for a moment, but then smiled. He met her eyes and said, "I think UnWoN created their own destroyer. But they also created someone who could survive that same destruction. I don't think a little water will kill him." His smile grew. "You're right about the opportunity for change. We're done here. The soldiers need time to question what they're a part of."

She looked up at her husband's closest friend. "And what do you think we should do?"

Rick put his hand gently on Marda's arm and leaned in before saying, "Let's go get Teran. And we can finish the job."

ABOUT THE COMPILERS

Cheyenne van Langevelde is a young author and musician whose greatest passion is weaving tales through story and song. Aside from writing and composing, she enjoys reading and collecting books, Irish dancing, eating chocolate, cuddling her bunny, and solving writing problems in the shower. She has two books already published: *Between Two Worlds*, (April, 2021), is a historical fiction standalone set during first century in ancient Rome. *Dìlseachd - A Stolen Crown*, (September, 2022), is the first in a nonmagical historical fantasy trilogy set during the Dark Ages of Scotland.

Instagram: thedancingbardess
Website: https://www.thedancingbardess.com

Nathaniel Luscombe is a young author from Ontario, Canada. He was first published in 2020 in a charity anthology. Since then, he has branched out and been published in several short story and poetry anthologies. He also has a novella out called *The Ones with Gilded Bones,* as well as two short stories, *Night of Teeth* and *The Planets We Become.* When Nathaniel's not writing, you can find him reading way too many books or hanging out with his large family.

Instagram: hecticreadinglife
TikTok: nathanielluscombeauthor

www.ingramcontent.com/pod-product-compliance
Lightning Source LLC
Chambersburg PA
CBHW071129010826
48975CB00017B/848